LOVING MY COWBOYS

BLESSING, TEXAS BOOK 1

LACEY DAVIS

VIRTUAL BOOKSELLER

❀ Created with Vellum

Two Texas Rangers and One Wild Bride?

Unmarried and alone is dangerous in the wilds of Texas. Lillian Bradley's family died leaving her to run the ranch that her lowlife neighbor covets. And someone is stealing her cattle. She needs a protector, a husband, and she needs him now.

Texas Rangers Will and Seth are looking for a gunslinger. They ride into Blessing, Texas just as a bank robbery is occurring. Only the thief isn't the feisty blonde woman they accuse. With one look, they know she will be theirs, that they will cherish, protect, and love her.

Is Lillian the key to finding their suspect and is she the woman who will satisfy their longings? Or will a family tie from the past destroy the life they're creating?

Want to learn about my new releases before anyone else? Sign up for my New Book Alert.

Sign up for my New Book Alert and receive a free book —
Blindfold Me.

https://www.subscribepage.com/laceydavis_author

1

Lillian Bradley sat astride a large red mare, gazing out at Texas's rolling hills, counting the cattle for a third time. Someone was stealing her cows.

With a sigh, her eyes roamed across the land she loved. All this acreage, cattle, goats, horses, and even a bunch of chickens, but they were all she had. Lily was alone.

Yellow fever had raced through her family, killing everyone but herself. Alone, she didn't understand how she had survived, but here she was with a large ranch and no one to help her with the many chores and responsibilities.

Some days, it was more than a body could bear, but she refused to give up.

Dust rose in the distance and she watched as a rider rode toward her. As the stranger drew closer, a groan rose in her throat. Jim White of the Big W Ranch, her neighbor, was coming for a visit. Rather an offer.

The man owned the largest spread in this section of Texas and was known for his shady deals, swindling, and even his prostitutes.

Pushing her long blonde curls back, her hand came to rest on the rifle she had become accustomed to being at her side.

He pulled his horse up beside her. "Good morning, Miss Bradley. How are you today?"

She turned and gave him an irritated frown. The wind blew her blonde hair into her face and she brushed it back. "Someone is stealing my cattle."

"I'm sorry to hear that," he said. "You know, a pretty young woman like yourself shouldn't be worrying over lost cattle."

"Maybe not, but yellow fever didn't give me much choice."

Her mare shimmied nervously, her paws dancing, eager to get away.

"Let me buy the ranch from you. Or even better, have you considered my son Matt? You are of marrying age. We could combine our land together into one big family ranch."

Like hell. She would shoot herself before she'd marry his weasel son.

"Thank you, but I'm not selling my family's land. Their deaths will not be in vain. As for marrying your son, no thank you."

It was all she could do to keep from screaming *oh hell no*. Not Matt White, a mean, cussing, tobacco spitting boy who knew his father would always get him out of trouble.

Mr. White's face turned red and his lips pressed into a thin line, but she didn't care. "A young woman should not be running a ranch."

"And yellow fever should not have killed my family." She sighed and turned to him. "For the last six months, I've taken care of this ranch and I plan on continuing. Need to find a new helper since Mr. Garza disappeared."

The man was like family and she was so disappointed he left her when she needed him the most. For nearly fifteen years, the man worked on the ranch and then one day, he just vanished.

"Miss Bradley," Jim said, his voice coaxing and gentle. "I could take the worry off your hands. You would be free to be the young woman you long to be."

It was true that she pined to have a carefree life again. One where all she had to worry about was helping her mother with dinner or the laundry. Where her grandmother baked a cake every week. Her grandfather and she went fishing when the weather permitted. But those days were gone. Stolen from her by a hideous disease.

"I'm so glad you came by, Mr. White. If you know anything about who might be taking my cattle, tell them I'm a fine shot with a rifle and I will not hesitate to kill them. Also, if you see my helper, Mr. Garza, tell him I would like to talk with him about increasing his salary."

Often times, she worried something had happened to Mr. Garza. Because she didn't think he would have left without saying good-bye. At least, she hoped not.

"Will do, Miss Bradley. You think about my offer. I'm willing to give you top dollar for your ranch."

Top dollar, her ass. The man was a known cheat and would not give her anything for the Sweet B Ranch. Over the years, her father had complained how when times got bad, Ole Jim was there to steal the property for little or nothing from the ranchers in dire straits.

"Good day, Mr. White."

It was a clear signal for him to leave. She had an appointment with the banker later today and she needed to be riding into town but would wait until he was out of sight. Though she doubted he would do something, she could see him setting fire to the house to force her to sell.

The man was a vulture of the worst kind. Preying on the weak and, right now, she was in his sights.

What she needed was a husband. Someone to help her with the ranch. To keep rustlers from cutting the fence and stealing her herd. Someone to fill the house with love and laughter. Someone to help her create her own family.

The big house was empty and creaked and moaned at night. Fear had her sleeping on the horsehair couch her mother had been so proud of.

While she had managed on her own for six months, it was time for her to fill her bed. Someone to teach her the ways between a man and a woman. Someone to scratch this itch she knew only a man could fulfill. And she wanted someone to love her and the Sweet B.

Today, she'd donned her prettiest dress. This morning she bathed, fixed her hair with the hot iron, and made certain she looked her best.

She knew what she had to do. After she went to the bank, she planned on talking to the preacher about any eligible young men who might be interested in her as a wife.

It was time to go husband hunting. It was time to find herself a man.

Seth

Texas Ranger, Seth Ingram, swayed in the saddle on the way to find the last member of the gang who killed his family. All the others had been turned in and hanged. This final man would complete the journey he'd been on since his teens.

"You know, Seth, once we find Calvin Smith, I'm thinking about finding me a woman and settling down. I know we've often thought of sharing a woman, but this way if you wanted to continue being a Texas Ranger, you could."

His best friend, Will Parker, rode beside him. For the last five years, they had fought and killed side by side.

Their horses plodded along the trail that led them to Blessing, Texas, where Calvin Smith was rumored to be hiding. This was their life. As Texas Rangers, they were sent to different areas of the state looking for criminals, men who had done something wrong. The worst lawbreakers.

"You're just horny for a woman," Seth said.

"That I am. But you're up for a promotion. This is your

life; you'll never quit."

As long as Calvin Smith was free, Will was right. Calvin was the last of the gang and he couldn't rest until they were all behind bars or swinging from a tree.

"I'm tired of this lifestyle. Chasing bad men, arresting them, and hauling them back to Waco. It's time to settle down with a warm woman between my legs, my cock buried inside her."

"Why not go to a whorehouse and find another woman. Maybe we can do that tonight."

It wasn't that Seth didn't long for a warm cunny to shove his cock in, just the thought made him hard. But if they were going to share a woman permanently, she would need to understand they were both her men. She would be treated with the utmost respect, cherished, loved, and fucked thoroughly.

As they rode into the edge of Blessing. Will's voice sounded frustrated. "I want more. Someone I know who will always be there. Who will bear our children. Aren't you tired of this life?"

"Some days," Seth responded. It was true. He grew tired of the trail, but his vengeance demanded he find all the gang members who slaughtered his loved ones. One remained loose. One last son of a bitch who would soon swing from a tree.

The town appeared a bustling center of commerce as they rode down Main Street heading towards the sheriff's office to check in and learn if he had seen their criminal. Seth knew he would delight in beating the shit out of Calvin Smith and hauling his ass back to jail.

From the barn, he watched the man shoot and kill his beloved dog, who had been trying to warn the family. At sixteen, he'd been a terrified kid who knew they were outnumbered as they shot his family one by one. Except his sister who hid inside the house that they burned to the ground.

As a grown man, he would delight in making Calvin Smith face justice for what he'd done that night.

"Look up there, people are screaming and running out of the bank."

"Bank robbery," Seth said.

They spurred their horses, galloping through town. When they reached the bank, they jumped off their horses and sprinted up the steps of the building. Just as they reached the door, a blonde woman came running outside with the bag of money in her hand.

"Stop right there, ma'am," Will said, reaching for his gun.

"No," she cried and muttered something as she continued to run down the stairs.

Seth shook his head. "Damn, she's a pretty one and I hate to do this."

He leaped onto her back taking her to the ground, he rolled her over. The sound of her dress ripping didn't stop him as he sat on top of her, grabbing her hands, pressing them above her head.

"He's getting away," she cried. "Stop the man running."

"You're under arrest for bank robbery," Will said, walking up to her.

"Get off. I didn't rob the bank."

"You have the money," Will responded.

Seth couldn't help but feel her shapely woman's body beneath him and he pressed his cock into her center. Damn, but she was one gorgeous woman and all he could think was if she wasn't a criminal, he would want to fuck her.

"Honest. I stopped the man. That's why I have the money," she said, struggling to get up.

Her movements only made his dick grow harder. He glanced up at Will. What now? They had never been in this situation before.

A man in a suit came running down the stairs. "Miss Bradley, are you all right?"

"Get these men off me. They think I robbed the bank," she said, her blonde hair in her face as she fought to rise.

"George Elam, President of the Blessing Bank. Miss Bradley stopped the robber. If it wasn't for her, our bank would be broke."

The man reached down and took the sack of money from her hands. "I can't thank you enough, Miss Bradley."

"Thanks to these men, your bank robber got away," she said.

Seth rose off her body as Will helped her up from the ground.

"I'm sorry, miss, but you have to understand how it appeared. I'm Texas Ranger Seth Ingram and this is my partner Will Parker."

She glared at them and then she glanced down at her dress that was muddied, a big tear at the waist. Tears filled her eyes.

"Oh no. My prettiest dress."

"Are you hurt?" Seth asked.

"No, I was hoping to meet someone later today and now I don't think that will be possible."

The banker reached out and gave her a hug. "Thank you, Miss Bradley. I've got to get back inside and settle everyone down and put the money back in the safe."

"Mr. Elam, we'll talk again soon," she said.

"Wait," Will said. "Can either one of you tell me about this robber?"

The banker shook his head. "Miss Bradley can tell you the most. She surprised him and hit him with her bag. Then she grabbed the sack of cash and when the other patrons started to go after him, he ran out the door."

"It's hot out here, gentlemen. I'm not going to stand in the heat of the Texas sun, but I recognized the robber."

Doubt crept in his mind. If she knew the robber, why was she running after him with a sack of cash?

"Is there a place we can get something to drink?" Seth asked. "We'd like to ask you some questions."

Not only to find out about the bank robber, but if she was involved. And if she wasn't part of the robbery, then he wanted to know more about her as a woman.

As much as Seth tried not to look, he couldn't help but stare at her torn skirt, that showed her petticoat. All he could think about was ripping that skirt off to reveal everything he felt when he was on top of her.

It was all he could do not to lift her skirt and show her how a lawman's cock could tame her wild ways. Why such an instant response? Why the need to ride her into next week or longer?

Maybe it was Will talking about the need to settle down, but right now, all he wanted was to show her how he and Will would cherish and take care of her. How they would make her the center of their world.

"There's a cafe across the street. We could get something to drink there," she said, brushing the mud from her skirt.

"Let's go," Seth said, taking her by the arm. A tingle of sexual heat flooded him. The image of her sucking his cock had him almost groaning.

3

Lily

What a day. First, Mr. White, and then while speaking to Mr. Elam, in walks none other than Calvin Smith and he tried to rob the bank. Did he really believe that stupid scarf was going to hide his face? She would recognize those eyes anywhere. They were evil. Pure and simple.

The man had come to the ranch three times trying to intimidate her into marrying Matt White, who had yet to show his face. They didn't want her, they wanted the Sweet B. But why was Calvin robbing the bank?

When she ran out of the bank with the cash, she had been trying to see where he was going, not take the money. The memory of the man sitting on top of her, grinding his man parts into her, sent heat flooding through her. Like nothing she had ever felt.

And Will Parker. The man's blonde curls and dark brown eyes had glared at her until they realized she was not the one robbing the bank. Both men were extremely handsome, and she couldn't help but wonder if each was married. She tried to sneak a glance at their hands and didn't see wedding rings.

All her carefully laid plans for finding a husband today were for naught. She looked a mess.

With Seth's hand on her elbow, he guided her into the cafe. With her arm at her side, she tried to hide her ripped skirt.

He led her to a table and they all sat. She watched as they both glanced around the room at the people, checking them out. For a moment, she looked around to see if she spotted Calvin, but he must have hightailed it out of town.

The waitress walked up to their table. "Lily, honey, are you all right?"

"I'm fine," she said, gazing up at Sarah Jane Wilkerson who ran the small eatery.

"So much has happened to you this year. And now this. We're all so thankful you saved the bank," she said. "What can I get you? It's on the house today."

"Thank you, Sarah Jane," she said. Though she had plenty of money, the bank was doing its best to hang onto her cash. Thank goodness she'd found her mother's hidden stash in a mason jar.

"And who are these fine gentlemen?"

She wanted to tell Sarah Jane to get to the kitchen, but instead she sighed. "Texas Rangers Seth Ingram and Will Parker. They arrived just in time to see me chasing the robber out the bank door."

"Oooh, welcome, gentlemen."

As she took their order, Lily couldn't help but gaze at each man. Seth was tall, her head would fit right below his chin. His dark brown hair was cut short, a long narrow nose, strong jaw, and mouth she couldn't help but wonder about kissing.

His lips were full, and she imagined them coaxing a response from her.

Will's deep timbre voice was demanding, yet his arresting dark eyes sent shivers through her. Blonde curls swirled from beneath his hat and his arms looked strong, foreboding, with strength.

As she glanced at their hands, she wondered how they would feel touching her flesh. Both men were handsome and virile, and she longed to be theirs. Shock radiated through her. She could only have one.

Which one would she choose and would he agree to marry her?

"Tell us about this bank robber," Seth said as his hand reached out and touched hers.

She licked her lips and stared into those gorgeous emerald eyes and wanted to become lost in them.

"His name is Calvin Smith. Several years ago, at the county fair, he got into a fight with my brother. Ben would have won, but Calvin threw dirt in his eyes and then I had to step in and stop him or he would have killed Ben."

She remembered like it was yesterday and it still pained her to think of how Ben had suffered at his hands.

"You seem to get yourself in trouble quite a bit. I can't imagine a man like Calvin refusing to fight because a woman told him to stop."

As he beat her brother senseless, she'd been terrorized. So afraid, she'd broken her father's law.

"He didn't. I had to pull a gun on him. I would have shot him too, if he hadn't stopped."

The men chuckled.

"Where does he live?"

"Don't know. It's the first time I've seen him in two years.

But I'll never forget the face of someone who harms me or my family."

Especially a man who was evil and only wanted to hurt them. She had no qualms that sooner or later, Calvin would force his way into her home. Especially now that her hired hand Tomas Garza was missing.

Seth ran a finger down the back of her hand, and it sent a shiver rippling through her. "Do you think he came back to fight your brother?"

"No, my brother died six months ago of yellow fever. Are you really Texas Rangers?"

"Yes," Will said. "We're actually searching for Calvin Smith. And since you recognized him, he may try to harm you."

She couldn't help but wonder if he wasn't the man stealing her cattle. It would be one way of getting even with her for interfering in his fight. But it seemed silly to come all the way to Blessing just to get revenge for a fight that ended with a woman pulling a gun on him.

"Someone is stealing my cattle. They're cutting the fence and taking them."

"What is your father doing about it?"

She licked her lips and gazed at the two men in front of her. Strangers and yet she felt at peace around them. She felt a bond with them unlike anything she had ever experienced. And they were so handsome, and even looking at them, made her heart speed up.

Just then the waitress set their food and drinks on the table. "Enjoy."

"Miss Bradley," Will said, leaning close to her, his hand resting on the back of her chair as he drew near. "What is your father doing to stop the rustlers."

It was now or never. For some reason, she felt a connection with these men and maybe she was wrong, but what could it hurt to try.

"My family–five members–died of yellow fever six months ago. My long-time ranch hand disappeared two weeks ago. I'm all alone."

They leaned back and gazed at one another before Seth drew closer. "You are living alone on a cattle ranch?"

"Yes, it's been in my family for two generations. My neighbor would love to steal it from me, but I've refused to sell. I'm not going anywhere."

Even so, that didn't mean she wasn't terrified. Some nights, she barely slept, hearing noises that she feared was someone breaking in.

"And now Calvin Smith knows you recognized him."

Both men's brows drew together and they frowned at one another. It was like they could read each other's minds.

"Yes. Today I came into town to talk to the banker who is not wanting to hand over Papa's accounts, though I have a will that says he left everything to me and Ben. The bank was robbed while I was there. Afterward, I planned to speak to the preacher." She paused and took a deep breath, knowing she had to say the words. Thinking they could be answer to her prayers.

"I need a man. I need a husband."

4

Will
The noise inside the cafe seemed to cease and a buzzing sound reverberated through Will's head.

She needed a husband.

Swallowing hard, he glanced at Seth as a smile spread across the man's face and he nodded. They had been friends long enough that he knew they were both thinking the same thing.

Color rose in Lily's cheeks and he could see she felt embarrassed to express her need. What she didn't realize was that she was their answer to an unspoken prayer. Will knew she was the one.

Lily Bradley was their woman.

Since the bank, he'd been thinking of how he wanted to remove that dratted dress from her body and explore every inch of her naked flesh. Sink his cock up to his balls into her sweet cunny.

But would she consider two husbands? How would she

feel about two men fucking her every night? Waking to being fucked every morning, starting the day with cries of pleasure. Ending each day with climax after climax.

With a sigh, she glanced down at her plate and picked at her food.

Seth signaled the waitress. "Check please."

"Yes, darlin'," she said and hurried off.

"Is there someplace we can speak in private?" Seth said.

A grin spread over his face. In private, he and Seth could explain to her how life would be with the two of them, and if that's what she wanted, then one of them would marry her today. And tonight, they would claim her, showing her that she belonged to both of them.

And whoever was stealing from her would face a cold steel gun barrel shoved in his chest. No one would harm their wife. Whatever the fuck was going on with her ranch, they would deal with the crisis and make certain everyone knew no one harmed Lily, their soon-to-be wife.

Lily looked confused. "We could try the church."

As soon as the bill was paid, Will took Lily by the elbow and led her from the restaurant. On the way to town, they had spoken about finding a wife and the good Lord had provided. Now they needed to convince her they were her men. Her protectors, her lovers, her husbands.

Two loving providers were better than one.

"Why couldn't we talk in the cafe?"

"We need someplace private. A church is not what I would have chosen, but it will do," Seth said.

She glanced at first Seth and then Will as they walked down the street with her sandwiched between them, protecting her. Right where she belonged.

The smell of roses drifted to his nose and his cock hardened. A quick glance at her chest and he almost groaned at the thought of her sweet orbs in his hands.

This was how their life together would always be. Lily between them, their cocks buried deeply within her. If she said yes, she would soon be crying out his name, begging him to give it to her harder.

The wooden sidewalk echoed with the sound of their boots as they all but ran down the street to the wooden building with a steeple and bell.

When they entered the church, they released their woman and removed their hats. A man wearing the cloth greeted them. "Good afternoon."

"May we sit here and talk for a few moments?" Seth asked.

"Of course," he said and disappeared. In the silence, they sank onto a pew, staring at the front of the holy building.

Lily's curious sapphire eyes gazed at them. The scent of roses, again, drifted to his nose. He couldn't wait to bury his nose in her cunny and smell her essence. She was what they wanted, but would she accept them?

"We want to marry you," Seth said. "You see, we don't believe in just one man, one woman. We believe in two men, one woman. That way if something happens to me, Will can be there to take care of you and our children."

Her mouth dropped open and she stuttered. "But I can't lawfully marry both of you."

"No," Will said, taking over. "You'll marry one of us, but we'll both be your husbands. We'll both take you to bed and we'll both take care of you. As our wife, we will protect, cherish, and love you."

"All we ask is that you trust and obey us. If you do not obey, there will be punishment."

She licked her lips, her blue eyes narrowed as she took them both in. "What kind of punishment?"

"If you disobey, lie, or keep your feelings from us, I will put you over my knee. We're men and don't always understand a woman's feelings. You must be honest with us," Seth said, picking up her hand and kissing the back of it. Slowly he released it and Will could tell he really didn't want to let her go.

With a tilt of her head, she glanced between the two of them and smiled. "I haven't been spanked since I was a child."

Seth glanced at Will and he knew Seth was thinking she was a virgin, an innocent in the ways of men and women. But not for long. Already his cock was eager to hear her answer.

"I own the Sweet B Ranch. Are you willing to help me with the cattle and the horses and everything that goes with running a ranch?"

"Of course," Will replied. "But that ranch belongs to you and our children. As Texas Rangers, we have our own money."

With a sigh, she slowly shook her head. "As much as I want to marry you both. How can you remain a Texas Ranger, help me with the ranch and not leave me? I'm so tired of being alone. Of having no one."

Will felt his heart wrench with sympathy for her. He understood and would never leave her.

Seth smiled. "Will is retiring. He wants a wife and children and he's a hard worker. The ranch will be perfect for him. I'll come home every chance I get. And if you're our bride, it's going to be hard to get me to leave."

She smiled and Will knew at that moment she was going

to say yes. Tonight would be their wedding night. His cock pulsed with excitement and he was ready to say *I do*.

Seth took her hand. "Lily, will you marry us?"

A grin spread across her face and she picked up each of their hands. "Yes. I'll marry you. But which one?"

Reaching into his pocket, Will pulled out a coin. "Heads or tails?"

"Head. Anytime," Seth said, grinning.

With a toss, Will let the coin drop onto the floor. In the light from the window, tails shined. "You have my word that I will never cheat on you. I will cherish our life together and honor you."

"Will you marry us, Lily, and let us be your men?"

"Yes," she whispered and grasped both of their hands. "I would kiss both of you, but that would confuse the father."

"Never forget you're ours," Seth whispered. "Will is your lawful husband, but you belong to me as much as you belong to him."

"I'm both of yours," she said, glancing at each of them.

A giddiness filled Will and all he could think about was tonight. They would claim their bride. "Let's get married."

5

Lily

Sunlight glinted through the windows as Lillian stood before the preacher ready to say the vows that tied her to Will and Seth forever. This morning when she left the ranch, she hoped she would find a husband, but never imagined finding two manly, handsome men to marry her. Not one, but two.

Right now, she didn't understand their life, but she would learn and do her best to be a good wife for them.

"I'm happy for you, Lily. After your family died, I feared you would never marry," the preacher said, smiling at her.

"Thank you," she said, realizing she would no longer be alone.

The preacher looked at the men. "Texas Rangers. Honest, good men. I'm so happy that you found a good man, Lily. Let's say the vows and get you on your way to a new, happy life."

For a moment, fear filled her. What did she know about these men? They were handsome and would protect her. They promised not to harm her. And she needed them.

Will ran his fingers down her cheek and a shiver of anticipation trickled like water down her spine. Tonight they would take her virginity. Tonight they would make her a woman. Their woman.

"All right, I'm ready."

The preacher began to say the vows and she trembled at the enormity of what she was about to do.

It was a new, different beginning from her old life. One she hoped would give her joy and happiness. A family once again.

When they finished the vows, Will leaned in and kissed her. It was a chaste kiss and she couldn't wait for a real kiss between them. Between her and Seth as well.

The preacher chuckled and then turned to Will. "As soon as you sign the book, you're free to go. I'm sure you're anxious to get your bride home."

Will smiled at the man. The three of them went into the office and they signed a license saying they were legally wed. She had a husband. A thought brought a giggle to her lips.

As they walked out the door, Will glanced at her. "What's funny."

"I'm married and I have not one, but two husbands."

He grinned at her and yet his brown eyes darkened with passion that caused her breath to catch. Now, she belonged to them.

"How far out to your ranch?" Seth asked.

"About an hour's ride. We need to get my horse and then get home before dark."

The two men glanced at one another.

Outside the church, they surrounded her, sandwiching her between them, their arms shielding her.

"You're ours now. I may not have married you, but those

vows applied to me as well," Seth said, his mouth inches from hers. Not knowing what to do, she closed her eyes as his lips brushed over hers. With a nip to her bottom lip, she opened her mouth in a gasp as his tongue dipped inside.

A moan escaped from between her lips and they broke apart.

"Did you hear that, Will? I made our bride moan."

"Such a sweet sound," he said as he spun her around in his arms.

His lips descended over hers and his hands cupped her face as he ravaged her mouth. Warmth spread through her and her cunny began to ache with anticipation.

When he released her, she staggered and they steadied her.

"Let's get home," Will said. "Our wedding night awaits us."

Her wedding night. For years, she dreamed of a church wedding with her family in attendance, but they were not there. With a sigh, she glanced at these two men and thought her father would have liked them.

Her mother would have been appalled. But they were her rescuers, her protectors, and now she had someone to help her.

They each took her by an elbow and together they walked down the street. They arrived at the stable and Will retrieved her horse and theirs.

Seth helped her onto the side saddle and soon they were riding out of town. When they were about a mile out, they pulled their horses to a stop and she halted.

"Why are we stopping?"

Will came over and helped her off her horse.

"Take your drawers off," Seth said.

"Why?"

"Because we asked you too," Will said, staring at her.

"But we're in the middle of nowhere. I don't want to take them off."

"You get one more chance. Take off your drawers, Lily," Seth said.

Why in the world would they want her to ride side saddle without drawers on?

Suddenly, Will dropped to his knees as he raised her skirt. He yanked down her drawers and she felt the hot summer air hit her bottom.

"Oh, Seth," he said with a moan. "She has the prettiest white bottom."

A swoosh of air sounded as his hand hit her bottom. "Will?"

On his knees, his palm connected with her bottom.

"We gave you the chance to mind us and you didn't. Now you'll receive your first spanking."

Swoosh, splat.

Heat swirled through her, centering between her legs. Her hands reached out and grasped his shoulders to hang on.

"Stop, Will."

He swatted her bottom again, but this time his fingers lingered, swirled around her ass, brushing between her legs.

Part of her was on fire. Her bottom burned and her cunny ached for something she didn't understand.

Again, there was a swoosh and splat, but this time when he finished, his fingers went farther. She felt them enter her cunny. Shocked at the rush of desire, she clung to his shoulders as he swirled them inside her.

Oh my, that was not what she expected.

"She's wet. I think our bride likes being spanked."

"No," she cried, fearing what they would think of her.

"Honey, it's all right," Seth said. "Spanking you gives us pleasure as well. Now kick the drawers off."

Her undergarments had piled around her ankles and she gingerly stepped out of them. Will picked them up and stuffed them in his saddle bags.

"No more drawers. We want you available to us at all times."

"But..."

"Don't argue with me, Lily, or you'll get more licks."

Stunned, she let him help her up in the saddle.

"You promised not to harm me."

"And we didn't. But you were disciplined for not obeying. We will never hurt you, but you must obey."

Marriage was not going as she planned. This was not what she thought it was about. But then again, what did she know? She witnessed her parents and grandparents. There's was a different kind of marriage.

Glancing at her two men, a shiver of want spread through her. She couldn't wait to get home. What else would they do to her tonight?

6

L ily

When they arrived at the ranch, the men nodded with approval, and a sense of pride filled her. This was home. Her family place and where she wanted her children to be raised. Their approval meant the world to her because she wanted this to be their home as well.

"This is nice. And you've been handling the cattle and everything all by yourself?"

"Yes," she said as they rode up the drive. She always looked for Mr. Garza, fear clutching her.

"How long?" Seth asked.

Licking her lips, she knew they would not be happy with what she told them. But there could be no lies between them.

"Six months. Yellow fever took all of them," she said sadly. "I've been alone except for my hired hand, Mr. Garza, who has worked for the family for fifteen years. Two weeks ago, he disappeared."

Will frowned. "Has he ever been gone this long before?"

"No. I fear something bad happened to him."

She watched as her husbands exchanged a look. Already she recognized they only had to glance at one another to communicate. Someday she hoped she would know them well enough that she could do the same.

"Look over there. A fence is down."

A sigh escaped her as she shook her head. "That place was repaired just last week. They've taken more cattle."

The rustlers seemed to watch her every move and knew when she would leave. It was her greatest fear that their actions would only grow bolder and thus the reason she had decided she needed a husband. And now she had two.

"Guess we're going to be repairing fence in the morning. For now, let's fix it to where the cows can't get out. Do you have any idea who is doing this?"

This was not how she wanted to spend her wedding night. But the ranch always had top priority.

"No, but my neighbor has been pressuring me to sell him the ranch."

"Tomorrow, we'll pay him a little visit and let him know we're your husbands now. Don't worry, Lily, we'll put an end to this."

A sense of relief flooded her, and she smiled at the men. How had she gotten so lucky? This morning she'd been dealing with the bank and suddenly her prayers where answered.

When they pulled up in front of the house, before she could get down, Seth was there to lift her off her horse. The ride had made her bottom even sorer after the spanking.

"God, woman, I can't wait to fuck you," he said when he pulled her close before he set her on the ground. "Get ready."

She swallowed. The words were coarse, yet they also thrilled her.

"First chores," she said. "The horses need to be put away and the fence repaired. Let's go."

Seth put a hand on her chest to stop her. "We are your husbands. You don't tell us what to do. We know what needs to be done around here. You go in the house and fix us a bite to eat. We'll take care of the rest."

"But…"

"Go, Lily. In the house," Will said. "You're a woman, not a ranch hand."

A smile crossed her face. She needed to let them take over the work. There was plenty to keep her busy in the house.

Thirty minutes later, just as she was finishing preparing their evening meal, they walked in the door. For a moment, it was a shock to see two large burly men standing in the main room of the house.

Just staring at them, she felt her body responding to their stares. Tonight they would make her theirs in every sense of the word.

"Wash up, supper is ready," she said, putting it on the table.

The two of them came over and soaped up their hands.

"Do you have a bathtub?" Will asked.

"Of course," she said.

"Good. I'd like to take a bath after supper."

She nodded and they all sat at the table. It shocked her when Seth said a blessing over the food. She hadn't expected that, but it was nice.

They ate in silence, the tension filling the air. When they were done, the men pushed back.

"That was excellent, Lily. Thank you for cooking for us."

As their wife wasn't that what she was supposed to do?

"My pleasure," she said, thinking of all the meals she'd partaken of alone.

"Let's talk about our marriage," Will said, gazing at her.

What did he mean? Had she already done something wrong again.

"Where is the bedroom?" Seth asked.

"My bedroom is upstairs and there are two others you can choose from."

Will laughed. "No, we all sleep together. The other bedrooms will be for our children."

Seth nodded and she swallowed hard. She would be sleeping between them. The thought was terrifying and thrilling.

"For the first week, you will remain naked in the house."

"What? No. I have to go outside and gather eggs and feed the animals and work."

There was silence and she knew she had once again disobeyed them.

"We want you available to us at all times. For the first week, I don't want to take the time to remove your clothes. We will take you whenever we want and wherever we want. If you go outside, you will be nude, so I suggest you stay inside or suffer a spanking," Will said.

With a sigh, she licked her lips. This was not what she expected. Nothing had prepared her for this. Had she made a mistake? She glanced around the table at the men and she knew they were hers. And she was theirs to do with as they wanted.

"It's going to take me some time to get used to being married and not in control."

They grinned at her.

Seth reached out and took her hand. "We want to make

your life easy. You married us to take care of the ranch and we will. Soon we'll go for a ride and you can show us the acreage. But for your safety, we want you in the house for now."

Will leaned back and gave her one of those dark stares that sent ripples of anticipation through her. "Tonight we're going to start your training and preparation."

"Preparation for what?"

Seth grinned. "Honey, we're going to take you in your cunny, your mouth, and even in your bottom."

Shock radiated through her. "No," she said automatically.

The look she received let her know she had once again misspoken.

"That earns you a spanking tonight."

"Let us teach you. Let us show you how we're going to pleasure you in every way. If something bothers you, let's talk about it. But first you must be willing to try," Seth told her, his emerald eyes reassuring.

This was all so new and frightening. Somehow she knew that tonight she was going to get an education she never expected.

Already she could feel a wetness between her legs at the very thought of the two of them taking her.

7

S eth

"Where's the bathtub?" Seth asked, his cock swelling so hard, he was about to burst. It seemed like hours since the wedding and he was past the point of being patient. Time to make their bride theirs.

But first, he wanted a bath. But he also wanted his sweet wife to bathe him.

"I'll get the water," she said.

Will laid a hand on her arm. "Where are the buckets? I'll get the water."

She sighed and nodded. It would take some time to remember they were here to take care of her. No longer did she need to do everything. As their woman, she would be treated with dignity.

"The well is right outside the back of the house."

Will grinned and walked out the door.

"I'll help you with the dishes," Seth said. It wouldn't take long and while the water was heating, they could clean the kitchen. And then he would take a bath and his lovely bride would bathe him.

In a matter of minutes, Will returned with the first couple of buckets. Lily and he poured the buckets in a large pot and hung it over a fire. Then he went out for more.

Seth finished drying the dishes and when Will returned with the last two buckets, Seth turned to Lily.

"Whenever we are in the bedroom or whenever we tell you to, you are to remove your clothes. Strip them off, sweet Lily."

Stunned, she stared at him and then she slowly began to unbutton her dress. The skirt was torn and he didn't know if she could fix it, and frankly, he didn't care. It was all he could do to keep from ripping the clothes from her body.

His cock was rock hard and throbbing and he couldn't wait to see her flesh. To suck those sweet orbs and twist her nipples.

The dress dropped to the floor and she stood in white petticoats, her corset lifted her breasts and made the tops spill over the silk material. Their woman was well endowed. And just the thought of licking her nipples generated a moan from him.

Will spun her around and began to undo the stays. "This thing can be burned. Never wear this again."

"But it goes well with my dresses."

His partner gave her a stern glare. "I don't want to see you in a corset again."

With that, he removed the garment and tossed it to the floor. She stepped out of her petticoats and stood before them in only her shift which showed her puckered nipples and the dark thatch of hair between her legs.

Tomorrow, that would be gone.

Will poured the water into the tub and Seth began to remove his shirt.

"What are you waiting for? Finish taking off your clothes."

Reluctantly she pulled the shift over her head as Seth reached for his belt buckle.

The sight of her firm pert breasts, narrow waist, and legs that he could hardly wait to feel wrapped around his back as he drove his cock into her, had him aching with need.

Quickly he removed his boots and then his pants and long johns. When he turned, she stared at his cock, hard with wanting her, sticking out like a sword.

Staring at her, he stroked the head of his cock. "All for you, honey. I can't wait to feel your cunny clinch around my shaft."

While Will shed his clothes, he stepped into the tub.

"Lily, honey, come here."

She walked over to the tub, her eyes large, her mouth pursed like she was frightened. "Would you get me a wash-cloth, towel, and some soap."

Like a frightened rabbit, she hurried over to a closet and pulled out items and returned. "Thank you. Now wash me."

Taking a deep breath, she reached into the tub and soaped up the washcloth. Timidly she trailed it over Seth's neck, shoulders and down his body, scrubbing him.

Will reached around her and played with her nipples, and she gasped. For a moment, her hand stilled.

"Don't mind me, keep washing Seth," he whispered as he leaned over her, his rock-hard cock slipped between her legs.

"You're our woman. And tonight we're going to show you what being with a man is all about."

She whimpered when his fingers found her cunny and he

began to stroke her clit. In some ways, he wished he was the one busy bringing her pleasure, but he also was enjoying his bath. The view of his sweet wife's naked body left him eager to experience her.

While he stared, she washed everything, but his cock.

"Wash it, honey. It won't bite and it's going to bring you pleasure."

Shyly, she reached out and swashed the rag over his cock, but then her fingers accidentally brushed it and she paused. She went back and let her fingers trail across the head and he thought he was going to die right there in the tub.

Seth grabbed her wrist. "Honey, I love it when you touch me there, but right now, I'm about to explode and the first time I come, I want to be inside you."

Her sapphire eyes grew larger and she swallowed nervously. Fear filled her gaze and he didn't want her afraid. He wanted her to be just as excited as they were. They would have to work at showing her how they could make her feel.

Seth stood, the water cascading from his body, his cock right at her eye level. "Where's the towel? I think Will wants to take a bath as well."

Oh, how, he wanted to push his cock into her sweet mouth and experience the feel of her mouth sucking him. But that would have to wait. Already she was as nervous as a kitten, and he wanted her to have a good experience tonight.

She handed him the towel and he stepped out of the copper tub, his cock bobbing, still hard as a rock.

Will stepped in behind him and he nodded for her to wash him as well. On her hands and knees, she took the same rag and bathed him. Seth toweled off, but the sight of her shapely bottom bent over, he was unable to resist. He placed his fingers on her clit and stroked it.

She moaned and pushed back against his hand as if she were searching for something, his cock. Oh, how he wanted to slam his cock inside her pussy. But this was not how they were going to take her the first time. This was just a warmup and soon, she would be begging them to take her.

This was their bride's first time and he wanted her experience to be earth shaking.

With her hands on Will, he suddenly rose from the tub. She handed him a towel. Still on her hands and knees, she looked up at him.

Seth helped her to her feet.

Will licked his lips. "It's time to make you ours."

"It's time for us to fuck you," Seth said, pulling her into his arms, wrapping around her naked flesh.

8

Lily

Walking up the stairs, nude, she felt like she was going before a firing squad. Terrified of what would happen and embarrassed at how naked she was. When they entered her bedroom, the men looked around.

"Honey, tomorrow, we're going to go through the house and see if you have a bed and a room large enough for the three of us."

"This was my childhood bedroom. My parents' room is down the hall, but I haven't done anything to it. My grandparents' bedroom is downstairs."

The two men glanced at each other. "We'll talk about that tomorrow. This will do for tonight."

She hadn't thought of how a husband would look at her bedroom. This room felt familiar to her. But she could see they were right. They needed a larger room and a bigger bed.

Will stepped in close behind her and Seth moved in front of her, the smell of their clean bodies, a fragrant aroma of manly man. Swallowing, she glanced up into Seth's face.

"I don't think I can do this. What if I want to back out? This is a mistake. I don't know you. I'm not ready—"

His mouth came down over hers, effectively shutting her up. As his lips moved over her mouth, Will kissed her neck, her back, his tongue trailing along her spine sending delicious shivers through her.

The kiss that Seth bestowed on her had her clinging to him, his lips consuming hers, his tongue sweeping the inside of her mouth as fire raced through her and she wanted more.

When she was completely limp, he broke the kiss and she didn't want him to stop. A growing heat blazed between her legs as she stared into his emerald gaze feeling like she was swirling out of control.

"At any time you want me to stop, let me know. As your husbands, we want you to want us as much as we can hardly wait to get inside you. If you're not begging us to take you, then we haven't done our job."

Confusion swirled inside her brain. They wanted her to beg them to take her? That wasn't going to happen.

His lips covered hers again and Will continued his assault on her senses as his tongue trailed all the way down her spine, reaching her crack. Then he pulled apart her buttocks and blew on that most private of spots, sending a swirling tornado of sensations through her all the way to her cunny.

"Will," she gasped, breaking the kiss with Seth.

Like a lamb being led to slaughter, she was placed on the bed with Seth at her head and Will by her feet. What was he doing?

Then she felt him spread her legs and look at her in the most intimate of places.

"Oh, Seth, she's got the sweetest little pussy. And I'm going to taste it."

Shock rumbled through her as he spread her innermost lips and he placed his mouth in her center and kissed her. Shockwaves of pleasure pulsed through her.

"Don't fight it, Lily. We're going to taste you in every way. And if we do it right, you're going to scream with pleasure."

A whimper escaped her as Seth placed his mouth on her nipples, sucking them into his mouth and nipping at the hard pebbles. A pressure was building inside her and she didn't understand what was happening.

And yet, she felt decadent with her legs spread, giving Will even more access so he could continue the pleasure he was giving her. This was not how she thought of a wedding night. This was not what she expected. It was better.

As Will's tongue continued to lick her clit, she felt his finger prodded at her back entrance.

"No," she cried as she gasped for breath.

Slap! His hand found her pussy and he slapped it hard enough to send a rush of feelings through her. She clutched the sheets of the bed. What was happening?

Slap!

"We are your men. You don't tell us what to do. In time, you will experience more than my finger in your ass."

His fingers were toying with her clit and she could feel a rush of heat, her essence coated his digits.

"I think she likes having her pussy spanked," Will said.

"Do it again," Seth said raising from her breasts.

Slap!

Suddenly it was like the world exploded around her and she clinched Will's fingers as he slid them inside her and she screamed her pleasure, the sound echoing in the room.

"That's it, honey," Seth said. "Come for us."

Slowly, the world seemed to right itself and she gasped as

Will stood and lay on the bed on the other side of her. Once again, she was sandwiched between her men and she liked the feel of their big hard bodies surrounding hers.

"Did you like it when I spanked your pussy?" Will asked.

What was she supposed to say? It seemed so unnatural when his finger rubbed her ass, and yet when he spanked her pussy, a rush of heat consumed her. Would they think she was a wanton? Was she?

"Answer Will, Lily. We're your husbands and you must be honest with us."

With a sigh, she quietly said, "Yes. Is that bad?"

They pulled her into an embrace between them.

"Not at all. We love to see you come. Whatever you enjoy is not wrong between the three of us. Now it's time for me to take your maidenhead. Be prepared for it to hurt just a little, but once it's gone, it will never hurt again."

Why did this sound so scary? And yet, she also was intrigued as to what else they would show her tonight.

Seth rolled onto his back and then Will lifted her and placed the entrance to her cunny right on top of his cock. She glanced down at the size and fear filled her.

"It's too big. It will never fit in there."

Raising just a little, Seth kissed her again on the lips, nibbling at her bottom lip, Heat began to swirl inside her once again.

"Honey, I'm going to make your pussy sing with pleasure," Seth said with a grin breaking the kiss.

With Will's help, she sank a little lower onto his cock and then she felt him stretching and filling her. For a moment, she didn't dare move, but then he gave a little shove and she felt the membrane give from the pressure. A gasp escaped her as she slid the rest of the way down to sit on his stomach.

"Now you belong to us. Never forget you're our wife. Ride my cock."

Was this what people had been doing since the beginning of time? The first few moments were awkward as she rose and slid down his cock, but then the friction between them began and she moaned as she felt her pussy clenching around his cock. Pleasure had her moaning, her breathing rapid and fast.

His hands were on her breasts and he tugged and pinched her nipples as heat flooded her body. With a moan, she closed her eyes and let her head roll back.

"Open your eyes, Lily. I want to see the passion in your gaze. I want to stare at you when you come."

Once again, she opened her eyes, her breathing was harsh and then she felt Will rubbing his finger at her back entrance then he slid his finger into her ass, swirling it around. How could something so depraved feel so good? She'd never imagined a man's finger bringing her so much pleasure.

"Don't come," Seth said.

How was she supposed to stop the rush of heat filling her, flooding her, and making her want to desperately find release?

"Hold on," he said. "I'm almost there."

She groaned and it was all she could do not to scream with frustration.

"Now," Seth said.

It was then that Will's hand landed on her ass, his finger buried deep inside her and she screamed as her body convulsed. Panting, she never imagined that what Seth said would be true. That she would be loudly proclaim her pleasure.

Drained, she slumped onto Seth's strong chest, knowing

that today, she had made one of the best decisions of her life. Marrying her husbands.

Will let her rest until her breathing slowed. "My turn, Lily. I can't wait to come inside your pussy."

How could she endure anymore? How could she take another round? And yet her body was already awakening.

"Watching you fuck Seth, I'm as hard as rock and ready to explode. This is going to be hard and fast."

What did he mean by hard and fast? He rolled her onto her back and pulled her to the edge of the bed. Then he lined up his cock with her cunny. He slid inside her, gripping her hips and lifting her to meet him.

Suddenly he grabbed her legs and spread her wide, opening her to his cock. In amazement, she watched as his cock slid in and out of her pussy. Once again, the pressure was mounting inside her and she clenched his cock.

In that moment, she knew what he meant by hard and fast. After having come twice, she was shocked at how once again her body responded, her muscles clenching around and gripping him.

"Oh, Seth, our bride's pussy is perfect. She's gripping me and I can feel my seed racing to explode."

Seth chuckled and leaned down and kissed her on the lips. The feel of his mouth on hers, the way his tongue glided over her lips and slipped between them, sent fire racing through her body.

Gripping the sheets, she could feel another orgasm building within her. She lifted her hips to meet his thrusts wanting as much of him as she could take.

Each man felt different. Each man's cock gave her pleasure and she knew she was about to come.

"Can I please come," she gasped between breaths, knowing she couldn't hold out much longer.

"Yes," Will said. "Come now."

This time the explosion raced through her, sending her spiraling out of control. Screaming, she grabbed the sheets to hold on while Seth held her in his arms, rocking her. Will stared into her eyes and she felt like they were connected as one.

With a grunt, he came. His seed flooded the walls of her pussy. He continued to hold her legs up as they both tried to regain their breath.

"Don't let it run out. Let's hope tonight we created a baby. A girl with your looks or a boy to name after Seth and me."

Stunned, she lay there for a moment. A child. Oh, yes, she would love if she became pregnant tonight. A family of their own.

9

S eth
Seth woke from a sound sleep. Lily was squeezed
between him and Will and they both slept soundly.
Her naked butt was against his cock and all he wanted to do
was slide into her waiting pussy. But something was wrong.

Outside, he heard a horse neigh and men's voices.
Suddenly a window shattered. His training kicked in and he
jumped out of bed, grabbed his gun and his pants.

"Will, wake up," he shouted as he ran downstairs.

It wasn't a rock as he thought, but a torch. Fire was
burning and he grabbed it and threw it back out the window.
Quickly he beat down the flames before he turned to the
window and fired his gun.

The sound reverberated through the night and the men
suddenly acted nervous.

Will came running down the stairs. "What the hell is
going on?"

"We got company. Bad company."

He peered out the window. Another torch was lit, reflecting the faces of three men. The man was about to throw the torch in the house. Seth aimed his gun and shot the man in the arm.

Screaming, he dropped the torch and Will fired at the second man.

In the distance, he could see two others driving the cattle through a cut in the fence. Suddenly a shot from behind them sounded.

He turned and there was Lily shooting a rifle through the broken window, naked as the day she was born.

"Now, that's a sight that makes my cock want to explode," Seth said.

She glanced at him and smiled. "Later, we'll take care of that, but now, we've got cattle to save."

The woman was headed toward the door and he pulled her back. "No. You're not going out there. Have you forgotten you aren't dressed?"

She looked down and shook her head. Then she walked over to the window and fired another shot.

"Lily," the only remaining man screamed. "I'm here for you, honey. After our run in at the bank, I think we should marry."

"That's Calvin Smith," she said, turning to look at them.

A rush of anger filled Seth and it was all he could do not to shoot the man. Taking a calming breath, he yelled out the window. "This is Texas Rangers Seth Ingram and Will Parker. You're too late. She married Will this afternoon. But thanks for letting me know you're in the area. I'm coming for you. Be prepared to hang."

"Fuck," Calvin said and they watched as he kicked his horse, racing down the drive in the darkness.

"Should we go after him?" Will asked. "He might get away."

By the time they would've saddled their horses, he'd be long gone. No, Seth had frightened the man, so let him stew on that information for a while.

"No, that will make him cool his heels. And it looks like the rustlers are going with him. Now who is he working with to steal our woman's cattle?"

They watched as the men raced out of the pasture and over the hill.

"In the morning, we're going to pay a visit to your neighbor. See if he has any clue who is working with Mr. Smith."

They set down their guns and Seth glanced at his bride. "You're not a bad shot."

Staring at her, his cock rose to attention. Even in the darkness, the woman's body was curved in all the right places. And he knew she smelled like roses and her skin felt like silk. And right now, he couldn't wait to get her back upstairs and fuck her.

She gave him a haughty look. "Living on a ranch, my father insisted we all know how to use a gun, in case of times like this."

Will shook his head. "We should have gone after him."

"And risked them circling back to harm Lily. I don't think so. She's in our protection now."

But how was he going to go visit the neighbors, unless he took her with him? Now, he completely understood her reasonings for finding herself a husband. And he had located the last man in the gang that killed his family.

It had taken everything in him not to shoot him this morning. But he would catch him and then the law would hang him.

With a sigh, Lily lit an oil lamp in the main area and then went to the kitchen. She came back with a broom. "That's the first time, they've tried to set the house on fire. Funny it came after Mr. White's visit yesterday."

Seth gazed at his wife. "Tell me about Mr. White."

As she swept up the broken glass, she spoke. "He is the largest landowner in the county. Maybe even in the state of Texas. Since my family passed away, he's shown interest in buying the ranch from me, even though I keep telling him I'm not interested."

"Has he threatened you?" Will asked.

"No, just pressured me. Yesterday was the worst. He even mentioned me marrying his creepy son. I told him no."

Leaning down, Seth put the dustpan in place for her to sweep the glass into it. They would need to buy replacement glass tomorrow. One of them would stay with Lily while the other went to town.

Now he realized the danger his sweet bride was in and it left him angry.

A quick glance at Will and he knew he felt the same. This morning's attack was a wake-up call as to the reason they came to Blessing.

The clock chimed five times. Soon it would be daylight. They would repair the damage to the fence and round up any loose cattle. Soon, he would be holding a discussion with Mr. White telling him the ranch was not for sale, and as a Texas Ranger, he would arrest any cattle rustlers.

And if that didn't do the trick, he had a Colt 45 strapped to his thigh that would guarantee there would be no more harassment of his bride.

Will pulled a quilt from the bed and covered the window.

In a matter of moments, they had it nailed to the frame of the house. It would do for now.

When they finished, they turned and gazed at their naked bride with a grin. Seth's cock was aching with want for Lily.

"Don't know about you, Will, but I think it's time to go back to bed."

He grinned. "Our sweet bride should awaken every morning to one of our cocks in her pussy. This is the first full day of our marriage. She should be properly awakened."

Lily glanced between the two of them. "But I'm awake."

"Oh no, darling, you've not been properly said good morning to yet," Seth said, knowing his cock couldn't wait to get inside Lily.

"Let's go back to bed," Will said. "Today, we start your training."

"Training?"

"You're going to love it," Seth said, picking her up and throwing her over his shoulder as he climbed the stairs. He popped her on the ass, loving the feel of her rounded cheeks beneath his hand.

The woman had the sweetest ass and it was all his and Will's.

"What was that for?"

"Just because I love the way your ass feels under my palm. You can count on more of that this morning. The sight of you, naked firing that gun, left me hard as a rock."

"Time to show you how we want to spend every morning with you," Will said, following behind Seth.

Lily giggled as Seth carried her up the stairs.

10

Will

At the sight of Lily being carried up the stairs by Seth, Will's cock had swollen with eagerness. He couldn't wait to shove his cock in her sweet, willing pussy. He couldn't wait to begin her training and he knew that Seth was of the same mind.

"Did you enjoy last night?" Will asked, wanting to make certain she had as much fun as it appeared.

"Yes," she said. "How often are we going to do this?"

They both laughed.

"Every chance we get, darling," Seth said. "How else are we going to see your belly swollen with our child?"

"Oh," she said startled as he dropped her onto the wrinkled bed sheets. Will lit the oil lamp sitting next to the bed. The sun had yet to rise, though the sky was turning pink.

"First, we're going to fuck you senseless, then we'll begin your training," Will said.

Seth quickly removed his clothes and Will did the same,

shedding their pants, their guns lying not far, so they could grab them quickly if needed.

"What kind of training?"

"Ass training, darling," Seth said. "So that when we both take you at once, you're ready."

Her sapphire eyes stared at Will and he could see she wasn't quite certain about their plans. "Wait. You'll see."

They pulled her up on the bed and Seth took his cock in his hand and rubbed it. "Darling, this morning, I want you to suck my cock. Wrap your pretty lips around it and suck the head."

Her mouth dropped open and her eyes widened. "No."

"Did you enjoy me sucking your cunny last night?" Will asked.

She licked her lips and frowned as she tried to sit up. "Yes."

"Now it's your turn," Seth said as he crawled on the bed, straddling her and placed his cock at her lips. "Suck."

Her blue eyes flashed in the dim light defiant. Will lifted her legs and slapped her on the ass. A moan came from her lips and he hit the other mound. Slowly she opened her mouth, staring at Seth.

"Good girl," he said. "Now give your husband pleasure. Suck."

Will watched as she licked her lips, her tongue going around the head and Seth moaned deep in his throat. "Oh, darling, you don't know how good that feels."

Behind him, Will held her legs up, her pussy glinted with moisture in the light and he stroked her clit. Slowly her hips moved as she she ran his fingers along her seams, stroking her.

Shoving two fingers in her, she moaned and raised her

hips to meet his every stroke. "I think you like morning fucking."

A groan came from her throat and he realized that their bride had taken all of Seth's cock into her mouth and he was now gripping her head as he moved his shaft deeper and deeper, thrusting over and over.

"No, Lily, don't close your eyes. Look at me. Know that I love the sight of your beautiful mouth accepting my cock," Seth said.

The sight of his cock plunging into her mouth was more than he could take. He couldn't wait to have his turn at her sucking his cock. Pushing her legs farther back, he slapped her pussy with his open palm and she moaned. Then he slammed into her cunny and hit the back wall of her womb.

She moaned.

With her pussy pulsating around his cock, he took his finger and stroked her clit as she sucked on Seth's member. Hard to believe they had been married less than twenty-four hours and yet Lily was theirs.

He would die protecting his wife and what they shared, he knew Seth would as well. Over and over, he watched as his cock disappeared inside his wife's tight pussy. Her dainty mouth sucked Seth's cock.

What a great way to start the day.

With her legs in the air, her ass was peeking out and unable to resist those white mons, he hit one cheek and then the other.

"Keep doing that. She sucks harder when you do," Seth said, his voice a moan.

Twice more, he hit her cheeks alternating, turning them pink, her pussy walls gripping his cock sending him closer and closer to the edge.

"I'm going to come, darling. Swallow my seed. Every drop," Seth said as he gave her one last shove, grunting as he came.

The sight of her throat convulsing around him, had him groaning. She had yet to experience complete pleasure. Seth pulled his cock from her mouth and she licked her lips, moaning as Will continued to drive into her sweet cunny.

Reaching down, he found her little pleasure button and twisted it between his fingers and her eyes widened. "Please, may I come."

"Anytime, sweetheart," Will said as Seth dismounted from her, but took her breasts in his hands.

He twisted her nipples which took her over the edge. Her pussy rippled around his cock and she screamed out her pleasure.

"Will," she cried.

The sound of her crying out his name, sent him over the edge. Caught up in his own orgasm, he groaned as his seed filled her, pulsating, coating the walls of her cunny.

The pungent scent of fucking filled the air as the three of them collapsed onto the bed, just as the rooster crowed announcing daylight.

The three lay there entwined arms and legs, their breaths loud in the room and happiness consumed him. This was the life he was dreaming of with a wife and eventually a family.

"Good morning, darling," Seth said.

Will chuckled. "What a way to start the day."

Lily lay there her eyes closed, her breathing harsh. "I'm worn out already."

The men laughed.

"And we're not done," Will said, knowing their girl would

probably resist what he had in mind. But in the end, she would be glad.

Rising from the bed, Will walked over to his saddle bags. Quickly he found what he was looking for. First, he took a wet washcloth from the water bowl to clean her sweet cunny. Seth sat up in bed and moved behind her, pulling her up almost into his lap.

"Spread your legs, Lily," he commanded.

Sleepily she gazed at him. "Why?"

"We're going to shave you," Will told her as he sponged her pussy, cleaning it before he began.

"What? Why?"

Seth held her and leaned into her ear. "Because we like a clean-shaven pussy, so we can eat your cunny."

Her eyes widened and she stared up at Seth.

"Will it hurt?"

"Not at all," Will said as he took out his shaving mug and mixed up lather. "Afterward, we'll make it good for you."

Lily spread her legs. With the brush in his hand, he ran it over her slit, bathing her cunny in lather. Then took the razor and slowly removed the hair, being careful not to cut her pussy lips. Down and up the razor went, removing every stubble, leaving her bare. "Oh my, Seth, you can see her pussy. It's beautiful and it's ours," Will said as he finished and wiped the remaining lather away.

"Good girl," Seth said in her ear. "You did that so well. Now we have more things for today."

"What?" she asked her sapphire eyes fearful, her blonde curls framing her face. Will's cock was starting to get hard once again just gazing at their bride, her legs spread, her bare pussy lips peeking out at him.

He held up the plug he purchased with this day in mind. A wooden dowel, narrow on one end and wide at the base.

"What's that?"

"It's a butt plug. It's going to train your ass to take us. Otherwise, we could harm you. And we can't wait for the two of us to claim you together," Will told her as he ran lube over the wooden dowel. "On your knees sweetheart."

"Is it going to hurt?"

"No, it's going to give you pleasure. Just like my finger in your ass." He could see the doubt in her eyes. "Once it's in, I'll show you how it will make you come. Up on your knees."

Reluctantly, she kneeled with Seth helping her. He pushed her head down on the bed and her ass was sticking up. Those beautiful white globes were just too hard to resist. He rubbed his hand over each cheek and then brought his hand down for a slight spank. Once, twice, three times. Not hard enough to hurt her but excite her.

She moaned and he knew she was ready.

Seth whispered, his mouth next to her ear. "You don't know how much I like hearing you moan like that and it pleases me so much that you like to be spanked. Someday soon, I'll make you come from a spanking."

Will couldn't resist running his fingers over her cunny and she was soaking wet. Their bride enjoyed being spanked.

Placing the narrow end at her rosy pucker, he pushed it forward, then pulled it back and pushed it again. "Relax, sweetheart and it will go in easier."

She took a deep breath and Will pushed it again. A groan escaped her, and he twisted the plug and she jerked in response. Reaching beneath her, he took her clit in his fingers and rubbed the nub as he continued to push the plug in.

"Oh, Will," she said with a moan.

Once it was completely in, he slapped her ass again and again.

"Please, can I come," she cried.

"Anytime, you did great," he said, pleased he had given his beautiful bride pleasure. He gave her one more slap on the ass and Lily screamed out her orgasm. He had never heard a more beautiful sound.

11

Seth

Later that morning, Seth counted the cattle, taking note of how many were missing. This morning at breakfast, Lily had given him the count. Their bride was naked in the house and he couldn't wait for lunch.

Will was stringing barb wire as they worked together to repair the fence. "After lunch, let's speak to the neighbor, Mr. White, and let him know Lily married a Texas Ranger."

The hot Texas sun beat down on them as they worked to repair the damage from last night's raid. Yes, there were cattle missing.

"I want to take a ride around the place. It sounds weird that Mr. Garza would disappear on Lily since he's worked so long for her family. That doesn't sound like a man who would ride away without saying good-bye."

"Agree," Will said, tightening the barb wire. He stood and gazed around the place. "This is a nice ranch."

"Yes," Seth said, seeing a cloud of dust coming from the west. "Look over there. What's that."

Cattle came into view along with three men on horseback. Seth reached for his gun. After last night, he wasn't taking any chances. Will did the same. They watched the men drive the cattle up toward the house.

Seth and Will jumped on their horses and headed that direction. Whoever these men were, they needed to know that Lily was no longer alone.

When the men arrived at the gate to the pasture, they opened it and ushered the cattle inside.

Will and Seth watched but didn't say a word as an older man rode up to them.

"Don't believe we've met. I'm Jim White," he said, glancing between the two of them.

"Texas Ranger Seth Ingram."

"Texas Ranger, Will Parker, Lily's new husband," Will said, sitting straight on his horse, his Colt 45 inches from his fingers.

"So the girl married," he said, shaking his head. "Parker, that name is familiar. Used to know a girl years ago with that name. Pretty woman. We planned to marry, but things happen."

Why in the hell would the man tell them about his past? To make them think he was a family man thus a nice man?

"My men found these cattle mixed with our own. They have the Sweet B brand on them, and we wanted to return them to their rightful owner."

"Thank you," Will said. "Appreciate that. We broke up some rustlers last night stealing our cattle. Even tried to set the house on fire."

"What? That's terrible," the man said. "It's a good thing she has a man here to help her."

"Yes," Will said with a smile that Seth knew didn't reach

his eyes. It was a decoy. A trick he'd seen Will use for many years.

"A woman has no business trying to run a ranch on her own. Glad to hear she has a husband. If you decide you want to sell this ranch, I want to buy it since it borders my property. I'd been asking her to sell since her parents died."

Seth clenched his fists knowing how this man tried to manipulate and coerce Lily into selling.

"Not interested," Will said. "You haven't by chance seen Mr. Garza? Her long-time family helper disappeared."

The older man shook his head. "That old coot was a drunk. I'm shocked he stayed this long."

Was there any truth in the man's words? Lily had not mentioned the man drank or was this just a way to keep them from searching into his disappearance?

"You wouldn't happen to know Calvin Smith would you? I'm almost certain I saw him last night in the darkness. We're searching for him."

The man's nostrils flared and his eyes darkened. "Never heard of the man."

Will nodded. "Just wanted to check. When we find him, he's going to jail."

"The Texas Rangers are the best," the man said sarcastically, and Seth didn't know if it was a compliment or condemnation. Either way, he didn't like the man. "Well, I best be going. Good luck, gentleman, with your search for Calvin Smith. Hope you stop those rustlers from stealing anymore of your cattle."

A feeling in the pit of Seth's gut knew who the rustlers were. Now they just had to catch them. "Oh, I hope they come back. We're ready for them."

"Be careful. I'd hate to see that young girl made a widow. But then again, my boy could marry her."

Those were not the words to say to a man who had just married Lily and already adored her. She was their woman.

Will's fake smile disappeared "Not going to happen. Lily belongs to me and I'll kill any man who tries to harm her."

Oh, hell no, it would not happen. Seth would kill this bastard before he had a chance to harm any of them.

The man laughed. "Don't get riled. I'm just worrying that something could happen to you and then she'd be left alone again."

The man's horse stepped nervously.

"That's not going to happen," Seth said, his voice ominous.

"We better get going. If you change your mind about selling, let me know."

Before Seth could tell him to go fuck himself, he turned his horse and rode out of the yard, with his two men following him.

"He's our rustler. This was just to make us think he was a nice guy and see how we felt about selling. He thought that if he terrified Lily enough, she would eventually sell," Will said.

"And now he's going to begin on us," Seth replied.

"Yes, we need to go into town and buy another glass pane to put in that window. And then we need to make certain we're armed and ready for a war."

"What did he mean he use to know a girl named Parker?" Seth asked.

"Don't know," Will said. "Mother never mentioned him. But then she never told me the name of my father, because she didn't want me to try to find him. If that son of a bitch helped create me, it would only make me hate him even more. Besides, there are probably dozens of Parkers around. Most not related."

Relief overcame Seth. There was no way to know if Jim White was his blood relation, but even so, Will hated his father. It wouldn't matter.

They gazed back at the house and then at each other. "Our bride is inside."

"Let's go," Seth said. "I'm getting hard just thinking about her."

12

Lily

Lily glanced out the window and saw the men talking. Her men didn't know how ruthless Jim White could be. Though they had told her to stay in the house and to remain nude, she couldn't.

She had to get out there and call out Jim's lies. She had to protect her men. Right now, it appeared they were getting cozy and that couldn't happen. Jim White was a crook surrounded by his ill-gotten gains and riches and protected by the law in town.

Her men didn't understand how capable he was of treachery.

Dashing up the stairs, she found a dress and put it over her nakedness. When she was dressed, she hurried back down the stairs and grabbed her gun.

The man was not going to win against her. And she would never let him hurt her husbands.

When she opened the door, there were her two men. They paused and looked at her and then each other.

"What are you doing, Lily?" Will asked his dark eyes narrowing, his mouth turned down.

Oh no. She glanced around them and saw that they were gone.

"I was coming to warn you about Jim White. Where is he?"

"He's gone," Seth said. "Why are you wearing clothes?"

She was in trouble and she knew it.

"I couldn't come outside naked, now, could I?"

"Didn't we tell you to stay in the house?"

There was a look on their face that she didn't like. One that left her uneasy. One that clearly stated trouble.

Will closed the door.

"Yes, but you don't know what kind of man he is," she said as they slowly walked toward her.

Will's eyes glinted with anger and Seth's face was drawn in a frown. They were furious with her and she feared she was about to get into trouble.

"I was coming out to protect you," she said.

They both laughed and then became serious.

"What did we tell you this morning?" Will asked.

She bit her lip and glanced at him, uneasiness filling her. "To stay in the house. But Jim White is a lying, conniving man who wants to steal our ranch."

"Not our ranch. Your ranch," Seth said.

"But we're married," she replied.

"Doesn't matter. The ranch is still yours. If you want to leave it to our children, that's wonderful, but it will remain yours. But you're avoiding the fact that you disobeyed us."

Stunned that they didn't want the ranch, she couldn't help but wonder if they planned on staying. "Does this mean you're not going to stay and help me?"

"Of course not," Will said.

"Lily, I enjoy being a Texas Ranger," Seth said. "But I would always return."

She took the two steps to Seth and wrapped her arms around him, hoping she could erase the anger from them both. "I can't imagine life without either one of you."

Her hand reached out and pulled Will into their embrace. "You're my men now."

"Who you disobeyed."

"Only to protect you," she said. "And to give Jim White a tongue lashing."

They chuckled.

"Take the dress off," Will instructed.

Stepping out of their arms, she unbuttoned the garment and lifted it over her head. "I only was going to wear it while I was outside, then I would have taken it off when I returned."

"Do you trust us?" Seth asked.

Though she'd only known them two days, she believed in them. They had already proven they were good men.

"Of course," she said.

"Then why didn't you let us handle Mr. White, who brought back some of your cattle."

What prompted the man to return her cattle? He was up to something and it couldn't be good.

Standing naked before them, she watched as Seth's eyes moved over her body. Then Will's.

"You didn't have all the information about what kind of man Jim White is."

"We're Texas Rangers, don't you think we've dealt with men like him before?" Will asked.

Oh, what could she say to that? Her men were strong and handsome and smart. Somehow she had let them down by not trusting them to handle that snake that lived next door.

"Disobeying you wasn't done out of disrespect to you. I wanted to protect you. You're my men."

Will took her by the arm, and they walked over to the couch, where he sat. Then he pulled her over his lap, lying her face down. Oh no, she wasn't going to get out of her punishment, no matter what kind of logic she used on them.

"What are you doing?"

"You're going to be punished for disobeying us. When we give you an order, we expect you to obey us. We're putting your safety before our own and we don't need you to protect us. Our job as your husbands is to make certain you are always safeguarded. When you disobey us, you will be punished."

Fear spiraled through Lily centering in her chest. "But—"

Smack, his hand came down on her naked buttocks and she felt the jolt through the butt plug in her bottom.

"Will," she cried.

"Count them," he said. "You're going to receive at least ten. More if you keep arguing."

Smack.

"Two," she cried.

His palm connected with her buttocks once again.

"Three," she said a little louder. The heat was building in her buttocks and she could feel the tears welling up in her eyes. She didn't want to cry. She didn't want them to see how much it pained her.

Will continued her spanking, hitting her harder than he'd ever done. Tears ran down her cheeks.

"Please," she whimpered, but he continued on, ignoring her pleas.

When they finally reached ten, she didn't move and he gently rubbed her reddened buttocks. Tears rolled down her cheeks and she was angry. How could what she'd done deserve this kind of punishment.

He lifted her and cradled her in his arms. "We are your husbands and we will protect you and honor you with our lives. You will want for nothing, but you must listen and obey us. When we give you an order, you are to obey."

She hiccupped. Didn't they understand, they were the best thing that had happened to her in a long time and she feared them being taken away. "But I wanted to defend you."

"That's nice, but we have each other's backs and you."

Seth reached out and rubbed her back. "We're only trying to look after you."

"I know, but I'm so afraid of losing you," she said.

"We're not going anywhere," Seth said, leaning down and kissing her cheek. "Don't worry, Lily."

But it was hard not to. Every day since the death of her family, she had faced danger and knew that threat had not gone away. He lived right down the road.

"Did that weasel offer to buy the land?"

The two men glanced at each other. "Yes," said Will as he rubbed her buttocks.

"Believe me, we recognize a lying, cheating snake when we meet one. But we have to be careful. This viper has money and he will use that against us."

"I know," she said, laying her head on Will's shoulder, her tears filling her eyes once again.

Being married was tough and giving up control was even harder. After all, she had been alone for so long with only herself to care for. No one had ever cared for her in the way her husbands were and she had to give in to them.

Still one man could take away the happiness she was feeling at the moment. Jim White. And that's why she feared him and was bound to defend her men.

13

Will
Will hated punishing her like that, but she had to learn that they would take care of her and protect her. She was the most precious gift they had ever been given and if she didn't listen or obey them, she could get hurt or even die. Just like days of old, they were her knights and she was their lady.

As the sun shone through the curtains, he laid her on the couch and stood. His hard cock strained at his pants eager to join with Lily. Slowly he removed his clothes and Seth did the same. As he pushed his pants down, his cock jumped to attention, curving toward the ceiling.

Rock hard and ready to fuck.

Lily lay on the couch gazing up at him.

"You're ours and we will defend you with our lives."

In fewer than twenty-four hours, this woman, their wife, had become everything to them. She was the rock, the foundation, they hoped to build a family life on. Anyone who would harm her would find them facing the barrel of his Colt. Lily was theirs.

And Jim White had no idea of the battle he would face if he continued to try to harm her.

Staring at her lying on her back, her legs spread, staring at him, her eyes dark with passion, he couldn't wait any longer.

Will kneeled and put his cock to her lips. She opened her mouth and took him deep inside, sucking on his erection, her tongue licking at the head. Heat spiraled through him and it was all he could do not to shove his cock down her throat.

Seth kicked his pants off and then he spread their bride's legs, hooking one over the top of the sofa. Kneeling, he kissed along her legs, leaving a trail until he reached the apex of her clean-shaven pussy. When he placed his mouth at the juncture, she arched her back, moaning around Will's cock.

"Lily," Will said with a groan. "Keep doing that. I love how she's moaning around my cock."

In a matter of moments, sweet pleasure noises came from their bride and he loved hearing them more than her tears. Her breathing hastened as she clutched at the sofa.

Gently, he pushed his cock in farther and gripped her hair in his hands. "Oh, sweet Lily, what you do to me."

His cock was deep in her throat and she gazed up at him, her sapphire eyes dark with passion, her throat convulsing around his cock. There was no way he could last much longer. Not with his bride sucking his cock.

Seth's mouth was again on her pussy, his tongue deep inside her, his fingers twisting her clit. She bucked like riding a wild horse and he knew she was close to coming.

With a final thrust, her throat convulsed as his seed shot down her gullet. She gazed at him, her need evident in her eyes as he came. Slowly, he pulled out and she licked him clean with her tongue.

"Please," she said softly. "Please let me come."

Seth's fingers found the butt plug and he gave it a vicious twist. She screamed with passion. "Now you may come."

Shaking, her body vibrated as she came, her voice whimpering as she shook.

With a sigh, she went limp and Seth smiled. "Not yet, sweetheart. We're not done. Up on your knees."

He helped her rise from the couch and crawl onto her knees. She glanced back at him. "Seth?"

"I'm going to shove my cock up your sweet cunny as far as it will go," he said, smiling at her.

She moaned and then he lined up his cock and pushed it in her dripping pussy.

He placed his hands on her hips, guiding her and then he began to pound into her, shoving his cock as far as it would go, fucking her hard. "Oh, fuck, she's so tight. So good."

Watching the two of them, Will could feel his cock getting hard once again. When Seth finished, he couldn't wait to do the same.

"Seth," she gasped. "I'm going to come."

With a smack, his hand connected with her bottom. "Not yet."

"Oh," she moaned, dropping her head and giving him deeper access.

Another smack to her ass and she squealed. "Seth, I can't hold back."

His thumb pushed on the butt plug and she screamed. "Oh, Seth, fuck me."

"Now you can come," he said as he gave one final shove,

his face tightening as he held her hips against him, his body jerking as his seed coated her pussy walls.

Lily gasped and writhed beneath him, her breathing harsh as her body spasmed with pleasure.

Seth fell back, his cock coming out of her cunny and Will stepped in behind her to take his place.

"It's my turn," he said, pushing in deep in her welcoming sweet pussy. The walls of her cunny gripped his cock, squeezing and wrapping it in a welcome sheath.

"Lily, squeeze me harder. Take me deeper."

Their bride slid down on her hands, her butt rising in the air, giving him deeper access.

Will gripped her hips with one hand, pulling her up against him as he slammed into her over and over. Then his fingers pulled the butt plug almost out, before he slammed it back in again.

"Will," she gasped. "Do it again."

Seth reached down and whispered to her. "Oh, baby, that's what we like to hear. We're so glad you enjoy us fucking you and can't wait until you're ready to take both of us. Soon, darling, soon."

His mouth covered hers as he kissed her thoroughly. She moaned as Will took her fast and hard, his cock plunging into her pussy. He reached around and twisted her clit.

Suddenly she broke from Seth's kiss. His fingers fondled her breasts, twisting the sweet nubs.

"I'm going to come," she cried.

It would be their bride's third orgasm, and this time, he was so close to coming a second time that he would not stop her.

"Go ahead, Lily, you may come."

The walls of her pussy gripped him, vibrating and pulsing and sending his cock into yet another orgasm.

As he groaned and held onto her for the ride, all he could think was that he was so grateful Lily had come into their lives. She was everything they hoped for in a bride and she belonged to the two of them.

Their seed mixed inside her pussy and hopefully soon they'd have a child.

Collapsing on top of Lily, Will rolled over until she lay between him and Seth on the crowded couch.

"Now, you understand why we want you naked," Seth said, rubbing her back.

"Yes," she whimpered softly snuggling between us. "I never dreamed being married could be this good. Please be careful, I don't want to lose my cowboys."

"Don't worry, we're not going anywhere," Seth said, kissing her neck.

With the afternoon sun shining in the windows, they lay spent on the couch.

Will glanced at his friend and smiled. He nodded in unspoken agreement. Their lives had improved. All because they married Lily. All because she needed a husband.

14

S eth
    Later that afternoon, Seth and Will made the decision not to go to town, but rather search the ranch to see if they could find any more of the missing cattle. They left Lily at the house with strict instructions not to step foot out of the house for any reason.

Unless there was a fire and then she could leave.

As they rode, they realized the value of the land surrounding the ranch. The green pastures, the river, the beauty of the rolling hillsides. There was plenty of tall grass blowing in the wind and water for cattle or horses.

"No wonder that prick White wants this land. Look at the river."

"The man reminded me of a snake oil salesman," Will said. "He's going to try something to get the land or Lily."

As they topped the rise of a hill, they noticed a horse with a saddle meandering in the valley below. That was odd.

"Buzzards," Seth said, noticing the ugly birds flying overhead.

They pulled their horses to a halt and sat gazing down at the scene below them.

"How long did she say Mr. Garza had been missing?"

"Two weeks," he replied. "If that's his horse, why didn't he return home?"

With a sigh, Seth kicked his horse moving down the hill. "Guess we better check this out."

As they rode toward the horse, he turned and neighed at them. Riding up, the mare seemed almost grateful to see them. The animal was not tethered like he feared, but rather stood patiently waiting on its owner.

At first, they didn't see the body, but the stench alerted them that something dead was nearby. Then they saw a foot sticking out from beneath the brush. His body half hidden, a bullet hole in his chest.

The body had been there for a while. They both reached for the handkerchiefs below their chins and pulled them up over their noses. When you worked crime scenes, you quickly learned what came in handy.

"How do we know if this is the man who's missing?"

"We don't, and no, Lily is not going to identify him. That would devastate her," Seth said, swinging his leg over his saddle and dropping to the ground. He walked over to the horse.

A beautiful red mare that neighed when he came near.

"Easy girl. I'm not going to hurt you," he said softly.

Will swung his leg over his horse, his feet hitting the ground. He walked to the body and reached inside the man's pockets. He pulled out a used billfold that held a wad of bills.

"Wasn't robbery," he said.

Then he found a letter folded up inside. Quickly he unfolded the worn missive and read it.

"It's Garza," he said. "This is a letter from his sister telling him about their mother's death. He must have saved it."

"The brand on the horse is the Sweet B Ranch," Seth said, running his hand over the horse's flesh. The animal quivered.

Stepping back, Seth reached into his saddle bags and pulled out an apple. The hungry animal gladly accepted the fruit.

The thought of her waiting for her owner left Seth sad. A sucker for animals, he didn't like to see them hurt. Since the death of his childhood dog, he couldn't bring himself to own another one. It hurt too much.

"The horse survived on the river water and grass, but didn't leave his rider," he said out loud, knowing the faithful animal would receive a full sack of oats tonight.

Turning from the animal, he made his way to look at the decomposing body.

"There's a bullet hole in his chest," Will said. "There's money in his billfold. I don't think he planned on dying."

Anger surged through Seth. Every murder reminded him of how his family had not planned on dying that night. How fast it all happened, and he couldn't do anything to stop it. Sometimes he felt like a coward for not running out and dying with them, but then his heart would remind him that he was left to catch their murderers.

"Look for a bullet casing," Seth said as he began to search around the area, needing to focus on the investigation and not his own memories. "Unless the shooter was a long ways away and accidental, but I don't think so. Looks like murder."

The two men tramped through the grass to search the area, spreading out looking for anything shiny in the weeds. Ten minutes later, Will bent down.

"Bingo, here it is," he said. "A Colt Peacemaker casing."

"Save it. It's going to be interesting to see what kind of gun Mr. White has," Seth replied.

"What are we going to do with the body?"

It was a question Seth really didn't want to think about, but knew they had to do something. "We're going back to the ranch and get a wagon and then return to take him to the house."

The law in this town was so incongruent that he wasn't certain he wanted to notify the sheriff of the killing but knew he must.

"I'm sure Lily will want to give the man a proper burial," Will said. "She's going to be upset."

"What about the sheriff?"

"What about him?" Will said. "Lily says he's corrupt. I say we file a report with the Texas Rangers. We can telegraph in that we found a dead man and that we're searching for his killer."

Seth shook his head, thinking this was way too easy.

"After we telegraph the Texas Rangers about the murder. Let's ask them to join us in Blessing. We'll tell the sheriff after we send the telegram. I'm thinking we're going to need some help with this case," Seth said, knowing if the sheriff was being paid by Mr. White, it would take more than the two of them.

"You don't think we can handle this alone?"

"Nope. Sooner or later, he's going to turn the sheriff on us. Then Lily would try to protect us. Every way I look, I see nothing but trouble," Seth said.

"All right," Will said. "By killing Mr. Garza, Jim White was pretty much assured of getting the ranch. Until we came along."

"That's why we need the help of other rangers. We're going to have a war on our hands."

The birds continued to fly overhead, circling waiting for them to leave. A sense of sadness overcame Seth. No, he didn't know the man, but from what Lily said, he protected and helped her at the ranch. No man deserved to die this way.

"This makes me even more nervous about leaving Lily alone at the ranch. Come on, let's get going. We'll come back for his body once we have a wagon," Seth said.

"Let's get some tarps to wrap him in. I know she cared about him, but I don't want her to see him like this."

"Absolutely," Seth said, leading Garza's horse to his own saddle and tying her to it. "Let's get back home. I don't like to be gone for long."

Now more than ever, he realized just how dangerous this situation was becoming. Jim White would do anything to get his hands on the Sweet B.

"Me either. Especially knowing that someone is trying to steal the ranch from her."

Thirty minutes later when they rode into the yard, Lily met them at the door, nude. Her big sapphire eyes stared at the horse. "That's Garza's horse. That animal loved him. Where is Garza?"

Seth took her in his arms and she started to cry.

"What happened?" she cried.

Will wrapped her back half in his arms. "We found his body. I'm so sorry, he was murdered, Lily."

"Nooo," she cried. "Why does everyone I love die?"

That was a question Seth had never considered before, but it must feel like that to her. Would it happen to him and Will?

"We're not going to leave you. No one is going to kill us," Seth said.

"Not even, Jim White," Will assured her.

But the man had an army of men, including hired guns. Now more than ever, Seth knew he needed to telegraph for help.

15

S eth
The next morning, he and Will tossed a coin to see who would go into town and leave the other one alone to comfort their new wife. When Seth won the coin toss, it didn't feel like winning. It felt like he was losing by being forced to go into town.

Last night, their sleep had not been interrupted by marauders, but rather their bride. They had fucked long into the night, satisfying their woman and keeping her from crying over Garza.

Now this morning, Seth was riding his mare into town while Will was at home fucking Lily and watching over the place.

As he rode into the town of Blessing, he couldn't help thinking the small frontier town was the perfect place for a gunslinger to take out a bank. Maybe he should talk to the banker once again, since he now had new information.

When he pulled up in front of the sheriff's office, he thought he heard shouting. He threw his leg over his saddle and dropped to the ground. Slowly he walked toward the sheriff's office and the voices rose in anger.

Opening the door, he saw two men standing before the sheriff, frowns on their faces. "Outside, mister," one of the men said, holding up his hand.

"No, these gentlemen were just leaving," the sheriff said.

"I can come back," Seth said.

"No," the portly man said standing behind his desk. "We're done."

The two men glowered at the man with a badge on his chest. "We'll be back."

"We're done and you can tell your boss that," the sheriff said, his hand hovering next to his gun belt.

Who was their boss?

The cowboys looked more like gunslingers as they walked by Seth. Suddenly the first one stopped and turned back to glare at Seth.

"Texas Ranger?"

Seth faced him. "Yes."

"Your partner married that girl on the Sweet B Ranch?"

"Yes," Seth said. He hated that he couldn't admit that she was his wife too.

The man walked right up to Seth and stared him in the eye. "Sell the ranch. Mr. White has been wanting that property for a long time."

Seth smiled at the man, his hand close to his gun. "What's your name? I want to put a name to your face, so that the next time you harass my partner and his bride, I can arrest you."

"Blackball Johnson," the man said. "Don't worry, Ranger, you're not going to live long enough to arrest me."

"Oh, even better, I can kill you," Seth said his fingers on his gun.

The men were gunslingers. Hired guns from the Big W Ranch.

"Get the hell out of my office, before I arrest you. And you tell Jim White, I said not no, but hell no," the sheriff said, his gun pulled and pointed at the men.

The man grinned and walked out the door. Though the sheriff was throwing them out, he got the feeling it was because Jim asked him to do something illegal.

When someone paid you money, they owned you.

"Sons of bitches, decent people don't exist anymore," the sheriff said, putting his gun back in his holster. "What can I do for you, Ranger?"

"Seth Ingram." Seth sighed as he shook the man's hand. Jim White's henchmen came to give the sheriff orders and he didn't like them.

Seth sank down onto a chair across from the lawman and studied him. Maybe the man wasn't actually on the take, but rather being harassed by the ranch owner. No, he was on the take.

"David Pettus," he said. "Sheriff."

"A couple of things. First, what can you tell me about Jim White?"

The man's hairy brows narrowed as he stared at Seth. "What do you want to know?"

"Everything, you know."

The sheriff leaned back in his chair. "Ornery as they come. About five years ago, he came to town and bought a small ranch. About fifty acres. Since then he has somehow managed to intimidate and threaten every ranch around him except for the Sweet B into selling."

Jim White was the worst kind of human.

"For over a year, he had been threatening Joe Bradley.

Then yellow fever hit and killed everyone at the Sweet B but Lily and Garza, their helper."

Seth nodded. This part of the story he knew. "Do you know where he came from?"

"Said Tennessee."

"Did you know that his men have been stealing Lily's cattle and harassing her? They came in the middle of the night and attacked night before last, but Will and I were there."

"I'm not surprised. He's hired some new guns. That's who was in here threatening me. The Sweet B is in danger," he said, running his hand through his hair. "Look, I don't want no trouble in town, but the man has an army working for him. And some look like hired guns."

"That's obvious," Seth said.

"Lily should sell to Jim White. Then maybe all these hired guns would leave town."

"Not going to happen," Seth said, knowing that he and Will would protect Lily and her ranch.

Like a bolt of lightning, it hit Seth. "Do you know if Calvin Smith is working for him?"

Seth pulled out the wanted poster from his shirt pocket and held it to where the sheriff could see it. "He looks familiar. Wait a minute, isn't he the guy who robbed the bank the other day?"

"Yes," Seth said.

"I know Jim White pays his men well, so why would he be robbing our local bank?"

Why did it feel like everything was starting to come together? "Don't know but I'm headed there to talk to the banker and find out."

"George is useless. Some say Jim has him in his back pocket."

A chuckle escaped from Seth. "Funny, that's what I heard about you."

The man shook his head. "I do my best to keep Jim White from owning this town, but a man with deep pockets, it's hard not to step aside and let him have complete control. What people don't realize is that he's bought up most of the small businesses. Much more and we will have to change the name from Blessing to White."

The sheriff was neither confirming nor denying that Jim White had him under his control. Yes, he'd witnessed the man arguing, but when you were bought and paid for, sometimes you were required to do a job you didn't want.

"Another thing I need to let you know about. We found Garza. Dead."

"Shit," the man said. "How did he die?"

"Bullet hole in the chest. From a Colt Peacemaker."

"A hired gun," the sheriff said. "With him out of the way, they thought Lily would sell. But that woman is as stubborn as they come."

Seth didn't say a word. But the sheriff was treading on dangerous ground. No one, not even another lawmaker, was permitted to talk bad about their bride.

"I'm here to capture Calvin Smith and take him back to Waco and if that means cleaning up the town, then so be it. No one is going to continue to harass Lily Parker any longer unless they want to face our guns."

"Whoa, I'm on your side and I would appreciate any help you can give me in cleaning up this town. Jim White needs to go."

Why did Seth get the feeling the man was talking out of both sides of his mouth?

He stood, needing to get out of this dirt hole office. "If you learn anything about Garza's killer, let me know. We're going to give him a decent burial, but that doesn't mean it's over. I'm looking for his killer."

"Good luck, Ranger," the sheriff said as Seth walked out the door. He got the feeling that Jim White owned the law in this town. He doubted the sheriff would ever look for the man's killer. And more importantly, why did he think that the hired guns were there to convince the sheriff to help them take the Sweet B?

As he walked across the street to the bank, he couldn't help but think back to the day they met Lily, running out of the bank with the sack of cash in her hand. He'd been shocked to see a woman bank robber, but then the banker cleared things up.

As he walked inside, his spurs jangling, two tellers sat behind cages helping customers and doing bookkeeping. The safe was behind them encased behind a large door.

"Is Mr. Elam available," he asked a man sitting in the lobby at a desk.

"Let me check. And who shall I tell him wants to speak with him?"

"Texas Ranger, Seth Ingram," he said, watching the way the bank operated and wondering how any criminal could think he would get away with robbery.

"Ranger," Mr. Elam said, coming out of his office. "Please, come in."

Seth took off his hat and entered the office.

"Have a seat," he said, sitting behind a big heavy oak desk.

"I'm just so thankful to you and Miss Bradley for stopping the robbery."

"The man that robbed your bank was Calvin Smith. Lily Bradley identified him. Can you tell me anything about him?"

The banker sighed and shook his head. "He's a hired gun that Jim White uses to intimidate the town folk around here. If you own a business and refuse to sell to Jim, then Mr. Smith pays your business a visit. A not too friendly visit."

That was interesting, but was it true?

"Was he trying to purchase the bank from you?"

"Yes, he made me an offer and I refused. Why in the world would I sell my bank to a man who would do nothing but run up the interest rates on the people in town? Also it would give him access to all the loans. He could force them to sell and take the land."

Seth had never considered that Lily might have a loan on the land.

"What about Lily Bradley, who is now Lily Parker. Is there a loan on her ranch?"

"Oh no, Joe Bradley did not owe anyone. That's why Jim White has not been able to get his hands on his land. The property is free and clear."

As Seth sat in the banker's richly decorated office, he wondered if he was telling him the truth. Both the banker and the sheriff had told him that Jim White pressured the ranchers to sell, even the business owners in town.

"Yet, Lily said that you refused to give her money out of her father's account."

"Yes, I was waiting for her to marry."

That didn't make any sense.

"But there was no husband in her future. How did you expect her to live, to eat?"

The man shifted uncomfortably in his chair and then he sighed. "Jim White said she was going to marry his son, Matt. That just any day now an engagement would be announced and that I was not to release any money to her."

It was all Seth could do not to punch the man in the face.

"Did you ask Lily if this was true?"

"No," he said.

"She could have starved to death because of you. There was no engagement. She told Jim she would rather die than marry his son. It was just his attempt to force her into marriage and claim her land."

The man nodded. "I realize that now. It wasn't until the bank robbery, an act to force me to sell, that I realized Jim White will do whatever he thinks is necessary to get what he wants."

Seth stood. "Mr. Elam, you will allow Lily Parker to withdraw whatever sum she needs from her father's accounts now."

"Oh, yes, tell her I'm looking forward to her coming into the bank."

Shaking his head. "Don't let me ever learn of you withholding funds from someone again or I will personally come in here and make certain that we shut down your bank. Do you understand me?"

"Yes, sir. Of course."

Seth turned and walked out of the banker's office. Why did people act like a fool when it came to other people's money? You would think the banker believed other people's cash was his own.

As Seth glanced at the sun, he knew he had about one more hour before he needed to return to the ranch. But first, he wanted to ask some of the business owners if they were forced to sell because of Jim White.

After he went into five shops and learned that all of them now belonged to Jim White, he'd had enough. Climbing on his horse, he headed back to the Sweet B, ready to see his woman and tell Will what he'd learned.

A sense of purpose filled him as he rode out of town. He'd been right to contact the Texas Rangers and ask for help.

16

L ily
Lily worried about Seth until she heard him open the front door and walk inside. Upstairs with Will, they were once again fucking, only this time, it was just the two of them and she missed Seth.

While Will was the brooding dark man, Seth was her light-hearted fun guy. The one who made her laugh at dinner and moan with ecstasy at night.

Will seldom cracked a smile and often she would see him gazing off in the distance as if he were watching a replay of something that troubled him.

The bedroom door opened, and she opened her eyes, to see her man. A soft smile spread across her face as Will filled her pussy with his cock.

A slap across her backside had her returning her focus to him, squeezing his cock. She heard Seth shedding his clothes and then moving onto the bed beside her.

His fingers reached out and tweaked her nipples, his

mouth covered hers in a kiss that had her melting into the bed.

"Seth," she moaned against his mouth. "I missed you."

"Darling, why did I know that the two of you would be doing this without me?"

"It was all Will's idea, not to wait for you," she whispered.

Smack, his hand met with her bottom and she sighed as pleasure filled her. Her husbands were now her life and she couldn't wait until they had a family. Children.

"You were the one who was naked all day while you cooked and cleaned. Shaking your breasts, your ass and just begging me to spank you."

"I did not," she groaned.

Seth slid beneath her with Will on her back. She was sandwiched between her men and a sense of rightness overcame her. This was where she belonged, with her men surrounding her.

"Well, now I'm home and I can't wait to bury my cock in your pussy," Seth whispered against her ear. "Feel you squeeze my cock and milk it."

Just the words were enough to spiral her closer and closer to the edge. "Me too."

Will leaned back and shoved his cock over and over into her. "I'm going to come," he groaned. "You can come again."

That was all she needed as her body vibrated and groaned and pulsated. She felt him drive into her one last time, holding her hips against him as he spilled his seed within her, coating her pussy walls.

Before she could catch her breath, they were switching places. Putting her on top of Will and Seth taking her from behind.

She felt his fingers on the butt plug. "Soon this contraption will no longer be needed. Soon we'll take you together. I can't wait to claim you at the same time, truly make you ours."

Gasping for breath trying to recover, Seth pulled it from her body, leaving her empty. She suddenly missed the feeling of being full. Of having something in her ass and in her pussy.

He reached behind him and picked up another one. "The next to the last one, Lily darling."

His fingers dipped inside her puckered rosebud twisting and turning as he slowly began to ease the larger plug into her bottom, rubbing her clit, tweaking that little nub full of nerves. Sending heat racing through her as she gasped for air, moaning.

Once again, she felt the fire building within her. She felt her need rising. Both men were different in their lovemaking. Each one giving her something she had never experienced. With Seth, she knew she would receive a slow, hard fucking that would leave her worn out.

With Will, it would be hard and fast and take them racing to the cliff.

When the new larger plug was finally inserted, he slapped her on the ass. "Good to go. Now I want you to cup my balls as I enter you."

This was something new and she did as he asked, listening to his moans as she felt his balls, moving them around in her palm, caressing them as he slowly pushed inside her. She was slick and wet with want for him and Will.

"Squeeze me, darling and I'll pinch your clit."

She did as he asked, his fingers sliding through her slick

folds until he found the little nub that caused her to moan as he pinched and rubbed it.

Will leaned took her breasts in his mouth, sucking and lapping at her nipples.

They were all skin to skin with Will beneath her and Seth behind her, his hand moved to her backside and he lovingly rubbed his hand over her cheeks. Then he slapped first one and then the other.

How could something that should be painful feel so good? Why did she want more? She turned and gazed into his emerald eyes filled with desire. "Do it again."

He grinned at her and instead of doing as she asked, he pushed on the butt plug. A spasm of pleasure rocked her and then his palm smacked one cheek and then the other.

"Seth," she cried, knowing she could not last much longer.

"Go ahead, darling. Come all over my cock."

Once again, he twisted the butt plug, turning it until she was moaning, the sense of fullness bringing her closer to the edge. Tingles of heat spiraling from her ass to her pussy as she clenched him and the plug, feeling stuffed. Would this be the way it would feel when they both took her?

Smack, his hand hit one cheek and then the other two times in a row and she screamed out as passion shook her body, her orgasm overtaking her, wrenching her from the inside out.

Will reached down and grabbed her clit prolonging the pleasure.

"Oh, Will," she cried, her body vibrating with pleasure. Her handsome, fertile husbands had her under their control. And already she could feel herself starting to fall for them.

They came into her life with a bang and she felt so lucky to be their wife. For without them, she feared what would have happened to her.

After she came, all she wanted to do was lie down on the bed and sleep.

But she could feel Seth still sliding in and out, and in and out, of her pussy. She clenched his cock as hard as she could.

"Darling, do that again," he groaned.

And she did, over and over, until she felt his seed explode inside her. With a groan, he collapsed on top of her back and rolled them both to their side. Will was right there beside her as well as she snuggled with her men.

Gratitude filled her as she thought of how she had been alone for so long and now she had these two men. She never dreamed marriage would be so good.

After a few minutes of heavy breathing with the smell of sex still in the air, she reached out and stroked their cheeks. "Do you guys know how happy you make me?"

"Hopefully as much as you make us happy," Seth said.

Will smiled. "Enough that I'm ready to fuck you again."

"As much as I agree with Will, we need to talk about serious matters. I've got information on Jim White and it's not good."

Will groaned. "Damn, but I hate it when you go all business-like."

Lily stroked both of their cheeks. "How about we eat the roast I have cooking downstairs and afterward, I'll suck both of your cocks."

The two men were jumping from the bed and then they reached back and helped her alight.

"Food and sex, what could be better than that?" Will said.

"You men can talk while I set the table," she said.

Seth's hand caressed her bottom and then he popped her there. "Honey, don't delay. I'm eager to feel your lips around my cock."

She grinned at him and then raised up and kissed his lips. "Seth, you make me happy."

17

Lily

The next morning, she rose from bed and hurried down to the kitchen. This morning she wanted make certain her men had a good breakfast before they left the house to confront Jim.

Last night, they lain in bed for hours talking about Jim White and the possibilities of who was involved in trying to take the Sweet B from her and who killed Garza. She had begged them not to go to his house, but being the Texas lawmen they were, they would not back down from a fight.

And while she respected that, she also feared for their lives. Jim would think nothing of killing her husbands in order to get to her. To take her land. At the moment, she would give it to him to keep her men safe.

But last night, they refused her offer to sell the land.

As she stood at the stove, a hard male body pressed against her back, a cock, ready and willing.

"Good morning, darling," Seth said.

"Good morning," she whispered as she turned in his arms and gazed up at him. "Are you hungry?"

"I'm always hungry for you. But food sounds good."

She smiled and looped her arms around his neck, moving her mouth over his lips for a kiss. Just the feel of him pressed against her was enough to make her want him again. If she could, she would use all her weapons to keep her men from leaving her today.

"What am I missing out on?" Will said as he walked into the kitchen.

The kiss broke and Seth whispered, "I was just thinking of taking Lily right here on the table. Spreading her out and eating her for breakfast."

"I'm in," Will said.

Would that keep them here? She began to remove her dress she was allowed to wear when cooking to keep her from oil burns. With a sigh, Seth put his hand on hers, stopping her.

"Honey, not this morning. But someday soon, I'm going to spread you out on that table and have you for breakfast."

A sigh escaped from her. This morning they were dead set on confronting Jim White. Quickly, she buttoned up the front of her dress.

She gave a nervous laugh, her heart wrenching inside. "The eggs are just about done. The biscuits and the bacon are ready or I would take you up on that offer. Sit and let me feed you."

"Hate to see good food go to waste," Seth said. "I guess we need our strength for today."

Terror ricocheted through her body at the thought of losing her men. They had just come into her life and she didn't want what they had together to end.

Last night, she had made it abundantly clear as to her feelings and they refused to back down. Whether she wanted them to go or not, they would confront Jim today.

Quickly, she dished up the food and carried them each a plate to the table.

"Eat," she told them.

Then she fixed her own plate and sat. They had not eaten a bite and were waiting on her.

"If no one objects, I'm going to say a blessing," Will said.

"Prayer is good," she whispered, glad to know they were religious men.

"Dear Lord, be with us today as we try to bring justice to the land. Protect us and guard us and walk beside us. Amen."

Seth glanced at him. "You forgot to tell him thanks for our wife."

"Oh, I've told him that every night since we married her."

Lily shook her head. "And here I feared you weren't godly men."

"No, ma'am. We were both raised in the church. Our children will be raised in the church as well," Will said, digging into his eggs.

Relief flooded through Lily. Yes, their life was not ordinary, but she was so relieved to hear their children would attend church.

"While we're gone, you are not to go outside," Seth said. "I don't care what is going on, don't step outside the house. Keep a rifle near at all times. If this wasn't a job for the two of us, one of us would remain here."

She licked her lips and hung her head. "For six months, I've been alone and worked this ranch. I'm not afraid."

Will laid down his fork and picked up her hand. "These men are bad. They're dangerous and we fear them taking you. They know you've married, so now they're getting desperate. Plus, if they could kill all three of us, then obtaining the ranch would not be a problem. This is one of those times, you need to obey us. We're looking out for you."

His words brought tears to her eyes. Why couldn't Jim White just leave them alone to live in peace. All she wanted was to raise a family and be a good wife to these men. And while she wanted to obey them, she also would protect their home while they were gone.

"He's right, Lily. Before they still had a chance at coercing you into either marriage or selling the property. Now, they know that's not going to happen. Don't go outside alone."

With a quick squeeze, Will released her hand. Staring at the food on her plate, she suddenly wasn't hungry any longer.

"Promise me, you'll come home to me. Promise me you won't let Jim White make me a widow," she said as tears filled her eyes. "I'm so afraid you'll get hurt."

Her men stood and walked around the table to her. They took her hand and raised her to standing and then they both wrapped their arms around her. Their hug sandwiched her in between them and she felt so loved.

Seth kissed her on the mouth. "Nothing is going to keep me from coming home to you, sweet Lily. You're our woman, our wife. I'd crawl home to you if I have to."

"Lily, we're good lawmen. We'll protect you, our children, and our home. We'll give our lives to make certain you're safe. Don't worry, we'll be back."

In their arms, she felt like nothing could harm their world. They were together, they were safe, and yet this tiny swirling doubt remained in the pit of her stomach.

"Be careful," she said.

"We promise," Will said as he turned her in Seth's arms and kissed her.

"I need my husbands."

They grinned at her.

"Time for us to go. Stay inside and be safe."

With tears in her eyes, she watched as they walked out the door. Soon they rode away from the ranch leaving her alone.

With them gone, she made herself get busy cleaning the kitchen, starting a roasted chicken for supper and doing things around the house. Anything to keep her mind off the fact they were gone on a dangerous mission.

She didn't trust Jim White and even if Will and Seth had a cavalry behind them, she would be worried.

Upstairs, she made the bed, remembering how they had played into the wee hours of the morning. As a young girl, she had never considered two husbands, but now she couldn't imagine life without her men.

The sound of gunshots sent fear spiraling through her. She glanced out the upstairs bedroom window and saw the man who robbed the bank, Calvin Smith riding around in the yard, firing his weapon.

"Oh, Lily where are you? I know you're alone."

What did she do? Her husbands said not to go outside and yet here was this outlaw who she knew would harm her if she did anything. How could she get rid of him?

"I'm going to burn down the house if you don't come outside."

"Like hell," she said, running downstairs. At least today, they had allowed her to wear clothing. If she'd been nude, it would have taken her time to get dressed.

When she reached downstairs, she picked up her rifle and then shouted through the broken pane.

"You throw a torch and my bullet will land in your chest."

He grinned. "I knew you were here. Saw the Texas Rangers ride off without you. You're alone. We could have some fun while they're gone."

"Over my dead body," she mumbled to herself.

He disappeared and when he returned, he had Garza's horse. The poor animal had been through so much. What was he doing with the mare? The horse was saddled and ready to ride.

"Come out or I'm going to shoot this mare."

There was no way she would allow him to harm one of their animals.

"No," she screamed. "Leave that horse alone unless you want to die."

Hysterical, maniac laughter came from him and then he rode over to the gate where the cattle were being held, opened it and began to fire his weapon over the cattle.

Without thinking she ran outside, off the porch into the yard, intent on stopping him from letting all her cattle escape.

"Stop," she screamed.

"Oh, so now you want to come out to play."

She raised her rifle and a bullet knocked the weapon from her hand. Stunned, she watched as his horse galloped toward her. Raising her skirts, she ran, but before she could reach the door, he jumped off his horse and grabbed her.

"Oh no, you're not going anywhere without me. We're going to take a little ride. Kind of like me and Garza took a ride. Only he didn't come back, did he?"

Fear spiraled through her. Calvin killed Garza. He was the reason her foreman was dead.

"He was my friend," she cried.

"Get on his horse," he commanded.

"No, I'm not leaving," she said.

"Fine, I'll shoot you right here." He aimed his gun at her and she knew she had no choice but do as he said. She wasn't ready to die. Her life with her husbands was ahead of her.

"Do you want your husband to find your body in the yard?"

With a sigh, she stepped into the stirrup of Garza's horse.

"All right, I'm going with you, but you better realize that when my husband and Seth return, you'll be a dead man."

"The only way to get the Sweet B is to kill the three of you and I'm just the man for the job."

Fear engulfed her and she turned her face away from Calvin. The man was crazy. Now it was up to her to stay alive long enough for Will and Seth to find her.

Unable to stop herself, she glanced back at the house one last time as he tied her hands and took the reins and climbed on his horse.

Her heart broke as she gazed at the place she had grown up and loved all her life. Would she ever see it again? Would she ever see her husbands again?

18

Will

As they rode onto the property, Will stared at the big house, the opulent barn and the signs of wealth that showed the Big W was a rich ranch. Cows mooed from a nearby pasture and Will felt a tiny bit of envy.

The Sweet B was a great ranch, but nothing compared to this one. Fine horses were in one pasture and another was filled with goats. Everywhere you looked, there were men on horses and they were all staring at the two rangers.

A cowboy met them in the drive leading up to the house. "Rangers, what can I do for you?"

"We're here to see Mr. White," Will said as they pulled their horses to a halt. "Tell him the Texas Rangers want to speak with him."

The man nodded. "Follow me."

They followed him past not one but two barns and then up a circular drive to a two-story house with white columns. A mansion set in the middle of the Texas prairie.

When they pulled up in the front of the house, the

cowboy slid off his horse. "Wait here. I'll let Mr. White know you're here."

After he went in the door, they turned and glanced at one another.

"Fancy place," Seth said.

"When you own half the town, I guess you can afford a place like this."

They waited, looking around, noticing the wrangler working with cattle, and a new building going up in the distance.

"Wonder what that's for?"

"My son," a voice said, coming up behind them. A trickle of alarm spiraled through Will. Since their last meeting, he had wondered several times if White had known his father.

His father had chosen not to be in his life, and it would remain that way.

"Sorry, I was in the birthing barn. We have some new babies arriving and I was checking on the momma cows. How can I help you gentlemen?"

Seth stepped out of his saddle, his feet landing hard on the ground. "We're searching for a Calvin Smith. Heard he might be working for you."

The man shrugged his shoulders. "Not that I know of. Ben, you know a Calvin Smith?"

The man's face turned into a frown, he took his hat off and ran his hand through his hair. "Not that I know of. I haven't hired a man by that name. Our men are locals. We offer jobs to the men in the community."

"Why do you want him?" Mr. White asked.

"Murder, armed robbery."

"Whoa," the foreman named Ben said.

"People in town told us he was working for you. That you hired a gunslinger. That true?" Seth asked.

The shopkeepers had opened up and told him about how Jim White liked to intimidate them into selling their business by using his hired gunman to threaten them. Not only threaten, but even pistol whip them into submission. Sadly, he believed them all.

"Now, Ranger, why in the world would I need to hire a gunslinger. People in town love me. They appreciate what I do for them. You've been sent out here on a wild goose chase. I think you've been had. Busy work is what my father would say."

Telling a Texas Ranger that he was doing busy work just to keep him busy never set well, and instantly, Will wanted to smash his fist in the man's face. But he remained calm and gave the man a fake smile.

"One last question, Mr. White. Do you own most of the businesses in town and are you pressuring the banker to sell?"

The man laughed out loud. "I'm a businessman and the town of Blessing has some good opportunities. I would love to purchase the bank. Think of how I could control the flow of money in town. But ole George Elam is a stubborn cuss."

Seth nodded. "So if we find Calvin Smith and he admits that you paid him to rob the bank, that would be a complete lie?"

The man shook his head and gave them a smile that only made his face appear evil. "Sure, I'd like to own the bank, but I'm not going to steal from it. Why would I do that?"

Will knew exactly why. In order to force the banker to relinquish his business. But right now, he wanted to hold all his cards close to his chest. Sometimes it was best to give your suspect just enough rope to hang themselves.

"If we hear anything else, we'll be back. In the meantime, if you see Calvin Smith, tell him we want to speak to him."

Like he would come and talk to them. Will knew better, but it never hurt to let the enemy underestimate you.

"Thanks for stopping by, Rangers. Hope you caught those rustlers who were stealing Lily's cattle."

Will would bet his next paycheck on the fact that Jim White was the rustler who had taken her cattle in his efforts to show her she needed to marry his son.

"Don't worry, we're watching for them. Oh, but we did find Garza, her helper's body. Somebody murdered him."

The man licked his lips. "What a shame. He was a good man. I really hate to hear that."

"What kind of pistol do you carry?"

The man frowned. "A Winchester. Why?"

"Whoever shot him used a Colt Peacemaker."

Jim grinned. "I'm not your man. Good luck with your investigation."

"You may not be our man, but that doesn't mean one of your hired thugs isn't the killer," Will said.

"No, but until you have more evidence, it doesn't matter. Now I think it's time for you to leave. Oh, and I remembered the name Parker. I used to fuck a woman named Parker."

Will knew the man was trying to rile him, but he would not smash his face as badly as he wanted too. It wouldn't matter if the man was his father. He would never claim to be his son.

"No one I know would be caught dead with you," Will said softly.

The man's face turned red as Seth stepped back into his saddle and Will did the same. Time to get out of here.

His gut was telling him the man was lying about everything, but his head repeated *find proof*. They needed to figure out a way to prove this man was taking over the town.

"Good day, gentlemen," Jim White said with an arrogant smile.

One that Will wanted to take a swipe at. But until they had further evidence, it would be hard to prove that he was behind the bank robbery or Calvin Smith or even attacking the Sweet B.

They turned their horses toward home as they spurred their mounts in that direction.

"We need to send a telegram to headquarters," Will said. "Something ain't right in this town and it's time to ask for help."

Will thought about their situation for a moment. They didn't have much, but they were certainly outgunned. Maybe that wouldn't be a bad idea. At least then they could get to the bottom of what was going on.

"All right, but let's make it quick. I want to get home to Lily."

An hour later, they walked out of the telegraph office and gazed at each other.

"Let's go home and see our wife," Seth said.

"I'm missing her pussy already," Will commented as they stepped into the saddle of their horses and rode out of Blessing.

"Are you going to tell her you're thinking of going back to Waco?" Will asked.

"I haven't decided yet. My cock is telling me I'm crazy and yet I haven't caught that last criminal."

Guilt flooded Will. He wanted to tell his friend the truth that he'd kept to himself their entire time together. He knew if he told, Seth would focus on the man and not the overall picture of everyone they needed to catch. But soon, he would tell him and then Seth would have to make a decision. But how did you tell your best friend that your half-brother was in the gang that killed your family. And how would he accept Will knowing his blood relative was the one who caused him so much pain?

"Let's get home," Will said, knowing he was keeping a secret and it was wrong.

An hour later, they rode in the gate and glanced around. The gate to the pasture where the cattle were kept was wide open and all the cattle were gone. The front door stood wide open and Lily's rifle lay in the dirt.

Something was wrong.

Jumping from their saddles, they ran into the house.

"Lily," Will screamed.

Seth took the steps two at time and raced upstairs.

"She's not here," he said as he hurried back down.

"Check the barn," Will said, rushing out the door.

When he hurried into the barn, he noticed Garza's horse was gone. Running back outside, he shook his head at Seth. "Someone's taken her. Garza's horse is gone."

"Calvin," Seth said. "While we were at Jim White's. He was waiting for us to leave, so he could take our woman."

Will cursed, his heart breaking. "Why would he want Lily other than to lure us to find her and then kill all of us. Why do I think that Jim White was thrilled to see us today, knowing that his dirty work would now be fulfilled?"

Seth checked his ammunition and then he looked at the hoof prints in the yard. "His horse has a bad shoe, making him so easy to find. Let's go. Our wife is in danger and we're going to rescue her and capture our suspect."

"Let's go," Will said, anger riding him hard. The man would be lucky to live through this. And if he'd harmed Lily in any way, he wouldn't live to see tomorrow.

19

L ily

Arrogant. Egotistical and not too bright was how she thought of Calvin, unless, of course, he wanted them to be found. Because he was making so many errors if he truly wanted to get away. As the sun sank into the western sky, she racked her brain trying to think of any way she could help her men when they came to rescue her.

Because she knew they would not be far behind. Once they came back to the ranch, they would see her rifle in the dirt and know she was in trouble.

It would be dark soon and she feared what would happen then. He would either rape or kill her, she knew. Somehow she had to last long enough that her cowboys found her.

"We're stopping right here," he said. "Time for me to stick my cock in that sweet pussy of yours."

Terror filled her. With her hands tied, she had nothing to fight with except her mouth and legs. And while it would not be a fair fight, she would do everything she could to stop him.

Glancing around at the area, it was wide open with sparse

trees and only a few scrub and cedar bushes. Not many places for her men to hide.

"No response?"

"Not worth wasting my breath on. You and I both know the rangers will come looking for me."

She hoped they were even now closing in on them.

"I certainly hope so. Time to rid the world of the opposition to joining the Sweet B and the Big W. If you wanted to live, you should have married my half-brother Matt."

"Wait a minute, Jim White is your father?"

"Yes," he said.

"But why the different name?"

"You ask a lot of questions. We're going to stop right here and then I'm going to strip you naked. Be thinking about me shoving my cock up your pussy and how much you're going to enjoy it."

She'd die before she let him rape her.

His horse came to a stop and she gazed at his back. Once her feet hit the ground, she'd be running. Even in the dark with her hands tied, she would do her best to get away from this crazy man.

"My husband will kill you," she said, thinking the man didn't realize that both men were her husband.

"Oh no, honey, my plan is to kill him and you. With both of you dead, the Sweet B will be available. Papa will finally be proud of me."

What could she say? With the two of them dead, the ranch would be available for sale and knowing Jim White, he would get it for almost nothing.

"Then your daddy, Jim White, will get what he wants."

"That's right," he said, stepping out of his saddle, she

waited patiently. If only she had something she could hit him with. A rock, a stick anything.

He walked to her horse and reached up to pull her out of the saddle. "Are you going to make it fun for me? Try to escape and then I can catch you and strip you?"

Well, crap! She didn't want to give him pleasure in any way.

"Why would I do that? I expect my husband to arrive any minute. There's no need to run. Will is going to kill you."

The man tilted his head for a moment. "What's Will's last name?"

"Parker. I'm now Lily Parker."

The man stopped his hands around her waist as he tilted his head. "My daddy knew a woman whose last name is Parker. I have a half-brother with the last name of Parker. It's been years since I've seen him, but I just wonder."

Fear clutched Lily's chest as her heart all but stopped and then beat at an irregular rhythm trying to catch up. No, no, no. Her husband could not be related to Jim White or even Calvin Smith.

"No way possible," Lily said, unease settling in her. Will had never said anything about his family before. There was no way fate would put him and his half-brother together. That was insane.

He lifted her out of the saddle and set her on the ground and then he turned to her and grinned. "Aren't you going to take off running?"

"See that cloud of dust in the distance? That's your fate."

She turned and walked away from him to sit on a dead tree not far from the horses. He glanced nervously in the distance. Her men were coming. Whether it was now or later, they would not let him kill her. She must have faith they would find her.

"No, it's too early. They would not have caught up to us by now."

A smile spread across her face. "They're coming. Are you ready to die?"

Calvin gave a nervous laugh. "You seem to have forgotten. I'm killing the two of you."

"Did you forget about Seth? He and Will are inseparable."

"Doesn't matter. I'll kill the three of you. Now take off your clothes."

"Kind of hard when my hands are tied. Besides you don't want to rape me."

He yanked a knife from his back pocket and sliced the ropes around her wrists. Fear raced through her, causing her to pause and glare at him. How could she stop him?

When she hesitated, he cocked his gun. "Do it."

"Or what? You'll kill me?" She tried to keep him talking to give them enough time to reach her. "About the time you'd get your tiny cock in me, they'll ride up and then how will you grab your gun? And my husband will make certain that your cock never works again."

His brows drew together in a frown and he glanced in the direction they had seen the dust. "See. No one is there. They're not going to find you until tomorrow and by then it will be too late."

A twig snapped and he whirled around aiming his gun in the darkness.

"You forgot to start a fire," she said. "There are wild boars in this area. They're killers. Are you ready to die?"

"Shut up," he said, picking up firewood.

The moon had not risen yet and it was almost completely

dark. Hastily he pulled out a flint. While he was trying to get the flame started, she quietly stood and began to walk away. He lifted his gun and fired at her.

"Sit back down. You're not going anywhere."

With a sigh, she returned to the log.

"Told you, you would try to get away."

"And I told you, my husband will be here soon."

Like an avenging tiger, Will charged from the bushes.

"Shit," Calvin said, standing and whirling his gun toward Will, but he hadn't planned on Seth launching at him from his back.

The man landed in the fire he was building, screaming in pain as the flames quickly took hold of his clothing.

Seth rolled him out of the fire, knocking his gun out of his hand while Will landed on top of him and punched him repeatedly in the face.

"You son of a bitch, I'm going to kill you," he screamed. "You took my wife."

Lily was so happy to see her husbands that she stood beside the three men, jumping up and down and yelling.

"Hit him, Will," she yelled. "Get him, Seth."

Relief flooded her. When her men left this morning, she wasn't certain they would return, but they came home unharmed and now had rescued her.

Finally, they had Calvin pinned and Will whipped out his handcuffs and slapped them on him. The man's face was a bruised and battered mess, his nose bleeding.

"You're going to jail, Calvin Smith," Seth said.

He grinned. "Won't be there long. The sheriff is being paid by Jim White, my father. I'll be out in no time. And besides, Will is my half-brother. He's not going to turn me in or harm me."

Seth reached out and punched him.

"Why did you do that?" Calvin said, gazing up at him.

"You're not his brother."

"I am," the man cried.

Seth and Lily turned and gazed at Will.

"Is it true?" Seth asked.

"Yes," Will said. "He's my half-brother. I haven't seen him since I was nine years old."

"That means that Jim White is your father," Lily said, feeling like someone had slapped her. She was married to one of Jim White's sons after all.

The man's fists clenched and his mouth contorted in pain. "Damn it, yes."

20

S eth

 In the glow of the fire, Seth watched as Will tied up Calvin.

When he finished, he stood over him shaking his head. "How in the hell did you get mixed up with Jim White?"

An owl hooted in the night, but Seth felt cold inside. The half-brother of his best friend was a murderer. Of Seth's family.

Nothing had ever come between them and he suddenly feared that Will would never agree to Seth turning him in. Yet, he knew the story of his family. Will knew this was the last member of the gang that killed his family and he'd kept it secret from Seth all this time. Why?

"We're kin," Calvin said. "Jim is our father."

"Jim White may have helped create me, but he's not my father. You and I both know what he did to our mothers. How could you accept his way of life?"

And Jim White was Will's father. How fucked up could

this get? Not only had his brother killed Seth's family, but his own father was trying to take their bride's ranch away.

Calvin sighed. "He's got money. Cash. I'm tired of being poor. Of working and never getting ahead. Dear ole runaway Dad has the means to help me get a head start. He seemed like a sure deal, only he's a hard ass. Even worse than mother described him."

Stunned that his best friend's family had been part of the gang that killed his loved ones, Seth stood there reeling from the shock. What did he do now?

"Yes, I see how much he helped you get ahead. Who put you up to robbing the bank?"

The man sighed. "It was a test job. A chance to show him I was serious about doing everything I could to help him."

"Help him? By confiscating the people's money so they were beholding to him for everything."

"That's not true," Calvin said.

Will shook his head. "Or a chance for you to get caught and hauled off to loiter in prison where you are out of his sight. He doesn't want the sons he left behind. He's got Matt."

In the darkness, something rattled the bushes. Some insect or critter scurrying away from the glow of the fire.

Calvin started laughing. "Matt is weak and crazy. You and I, we're strong. You should join us, Will. You and I working for Pops, we would have him owning this county in no time."

Anger rippled like an earthquake through Seth. Over his dead body would the two of them join up with Jim White. No way would he accept his best friend joining with his ruthless father. And Calvin would hang for the crimes committed against Seth's family.

Even in the darkness, Seth could see Will's hands shook

with rage. Maybe his friend was not being swayed to the dark side. Maybe their friendship still had hope.

"No, it's wrong. I could never respect or love that man. He left my seventeen-year-old mother pregnant and alone. He did the same to your mother. How can you forgive him? An honest man doesn't walk out on his pregnant fiancée."

The words were said with such venom, you would think Calvin was about to get rattlesnake bit.

The man sighed. "Maybe my mother was to blame. Why did she get involved with a man like Jim? I wouldn't have been born if she'd keep her knickers up and her legs together. What about your own mother?"

Seth could see his friend's veins popping out on his face and feared him losing control and yet his own anger simmered below the surface, like a snake coiled and ready to strike.

"My mother believed he was going to marry her. He forced her to have sex with him before the wedding. They had chosen a date and time and then he learned she was pregnant. And he ran like the coward he is. He may have money, but that doesn't mean he's not a yellowed belly viper."

Seth had never heard how his mother got pregnant. Only knew Will was the product of a wedding that didn't happen. An illegitimate child who grew up without a father. His mother worked two and three jobs to support them.

The sound of a log popping on the fire was the only sound heard in the camp. Seth turned and gazed at Lily who stood watching, her eyes wide with fright, her face taut with tension.

Will turned and walked into the darkness, leaving their prisoner tied up lying on the ground. Right now, the man needed to fight the demons in his soul.

And Seth said a silent prayer that the man he considered a brother, his friend, would come out the winner.

Lily ran after Will into the darkness leaving Seth alone with Calvin. It was all he could do not to pull out his gun and shoot the bastard. But he had sworn an oath to protect the citizens of Texas and abide by the law.

Cold-blooded murder was not acceptable.

Calvin struggled on the ground. "Ants are crawling on me. Could someone help me sit up or at least give me my blanket."

Though the man deserved to be riddled with fire ant bites, Seth realized as a man of the law, he had to be above his own personal feelings. He went to the man's horse and pulled out a blanket. He tossed it to him and Calvin managed to sit up and maneuver the blanket beneath him.

"Were you ever a member of the Mercardo Gang?"

The man's head swiveled and he glanced at Seth, his eyes narrowed. "Why you asking?"

"Because they killed my family. The Lazy I ranch on the night of June 21, 1871. You were there that night. I saw you. I've captured every gang member, but you," Seth said as he glared at the man. "You may think that because your brother is a Texas Ranger, you're going to get a break. No way in hell will you ever get out of prison once I'm done with you."

The man turned his head. "Did you have a younger sister?"

"Yes."

"I enjoyed fucking her."

Seth lunged at Calvin, rage roaring in his head. But then the grin on Calvin's face calmed him.

"You didn't fuck her. She died in the house fire," he said.

"She burned to death because someone believed my father had gold coins. He was a simple farmer. He had nothing."

His confirmation of being there sent hate spiraling through Seth and he had to take a deep breath to keep from killing the man.

"You're going to hang. You are the last member of the gang. All the others I've caught. You're the last to die."

There was silence as Seth walked away from the man on the ground. He needed to put distance between them or else he feared he would kill this monster who set his family farm on fire.

He still didn't understand the reason. Though Frank Mercardo said some idiot thought his father was holding gold coins from the war. But it was all a lie. A lie that killed innocent people and left him scared.

Just a boy, he had hidden in the outhouse, terrified, while his family was shot and killed in the front yard and the house set on fire. Only his sister had hidden, and in the end, she died too.

Now they were gone and he was alone except for Will and Lily. And yet, how did the knowledge that Calvin was Will's brother affect their relationship?

Because there was no way Calvin could escape justice, regardless of the fact that he was Will's brother.

Seth would make certain the man would hang.

What did they do now?

21

Lily

Lily hurried in the darkness after Will. She'd seen his face, the way he looked like he wanted to murder his brother. And yet, part of her was fearful. Will was Jim White's son.

She walked up behind him and he whirled around, his hand on his gun. "It's me."

He didn't say anything but continued to stare out into the darkness.

"I hate him," he said, his voice cracking. "For what he did to my mother. For how he abandoned me. For the evil I see in his eyes."

She laid her hand on his arm. "You're not him."

"No, but his blood pulses in me. What if suddenly I become like him. What if I become greedy and selfish and turn into my father?"

Lily slid her arms around his waist and pulled him tightly to her. "You'll never be like him. Your mother taught you well.

You are an honest, lawful man who would help anyone. You are not your father."

Suddenly he turned and pulled her into his arms and held her. She could feel him shaking.

"When people learn that he's my father, they're going to think I'm like him."

"Then they will be wrong."

"And you're married to me. My tainted blood will hurt you and our children. What if he suddenly wants to be their grandfather. I don't want anything to do with him."

Relief flooded her when he said he wanted nothing to do with the man, as she thought of Jim wanting to be a grandfather to her children. Absolutely not! Over her dead body and she knew he could arrange that.

"Did you know that Jim White was your father?"

"No, I knew Calvin was my half-brother. When I was nine, our mothers met and talked and we were introduced. But I had no idea Jim White fathered us both. I haven't seen Calvin since that day."

"Maybe he's not? Maybe this is all a big lie. After all, you don't have his name and neither does Calvin."

Oh, how she wanted that to be true for Will, but right now, she knew he needed her reassurance, her support.

"That's because we were both illegitimate. He never married our mothers. Why should he? He didn't want a family, but rather a woman to satisfy his needs. Before I left home, my mother made me promise I would never do to a woman what he did to her. That's why I insisted on marrying you before we had sex. No child of mine will ever be illegitimate."

It all made sense, except for how Calvin found Jim White

and was he using the man to get what he wanted? Or was Jim White using him?

"Strange how you became a Texas Ranger and Calvin an outlaw."

Suddenly Will tensed and began to curse.

"What's wrong?"

"Seth," he said. "He didn't know that Calvin was my half-brother. I never told him because I didn't want it to ruin our friendship. How could I be so stupid. He deserved to know the truth."

Lily stared at him in the darkness. "Why will he care?"

With a sigh, Will laid his head on her shoulder and wrapped her in his arms. "Because my brother was in a gang that killed Seth's family. He's caught them all but Calvin."

Fear spiraled through Lily. Why didn't she know these things? Sure, they had been married for less than a week, but she should have asked about her husbands' backgrounds. Instead they had focused on each other.

And now to learn that Will's half-brother had killed Seth's family, she didn't know how that would affect their relationship. She loved her men and prayed they could put this behind them.

Just then, the sound of a twig snapping alerted Lily that Seth had followed them.

"You all right, Will?"

"No, I'm not. That son of a bitch is my father. But even worse, my brother was part responsible for murdering your family. My best friend. If I could go back in time, I would give my life to save your family."

In the darkness, Lily watched as Seth wiped a tear from his eye and she realized the pain he felt.

"Thank you, Will. Promise me you won't keep any other secrets from us."

"Seth, I wasn't even certain it was the same man. But you're right, I should have told you. But that would mean facing the fact that my half-brother was an evil criminal. Someone who killed my best friend's family."

There was silence and Lily reached out in the darkness and drew Seth to her. "You are part of our family. The three of us are family. We're all each other has."

It was true. Lily's family was gone, Seth's family was gone, and even Will's mother had died several years ago. They were all they had. And it was enough.

"It's true. But I'm not going to give your half-brother any special treatment. He will be taken to Waco, just like all the other gang members and there he will stand trial."

Will reached out and took his friend's hand. They were standing in a circle, all three of them holding hands. "That's what I expect. He must pay for what he did. Believe me, there is no love lost between us."

"What about your father?" Seth asked.

"I don't have a father and want nothing to do with any man who tries to claim me as their son. He gave me life, but he's not my father. Both of you promise me that if something ever happens to me, that our children know that I love them and that I am their father. No child should ever suffer because their father doesn't want them."

They moved together, giving each other a hug, with Lily between them.

"You have my word," Seth said.

"Mine too," Lily answered.

For a moment, they simply stood there and held one another.

"What are we going to do about Jim White?" Seth said. "I can't go off and leave you, until I know you're safe."

Lily stiffened in his arms. "Leave us? Where are you going?"

"Honey, I am a Texas Ranger. I'm up for a promotion. Sooner or later, I must return to Waco and my job."

It was the first she had heard about him leaving and she didn't like it one bit. Not at all. They had just found each other and she didn't want him to go. And how long would he be gone?

"No, I want you here with me and Will." Then she whirled and faced Will. "Are you leaving too?"

"No, I'm quitting to stay here by your side. This is what I want, Lily." He gazed at Seth. "After the last week, I hoped you would change your mind. Especially now that you've caught everyone who killed your family."

Lily whirled to gaze in the darkness at Seth. She wrapped her arms around him and pressed her body to his. "Stay and help Will run the ranch."

He leaned down and kissed her on the mouth. "I'll think about it."

22

Will

The next morning, they all rode into the town of Blessing. Seth had the reins of Calvin's horse as he pulled it along with the man's hands tied to the saddle horn. Will and Lily rode behind the two of them.

It was early, sun was up, but the streets were empty. What the hell was going on? Main street curved toward the sheriff's office and they were met by a blockade in the street. From behind liquor barrels, five guns were aimed at them.

The sheriff waved at them. "Get down off your horses."

"Sheriff," Seth said, "what's going on?"

"You're under arrest for the murder of Tomas Garza," he said, grinning.

"That's a lie," Lily said, jumping down from her horse and approaching the man.

The sound of rifles turning on her, and triggers being cocked sent a chill through Will. What the hell was she doing?

"Gentleman, you really don't want to kill my wife, because I will kill every one of you. Lily, step back," he said calmly.

Slowly she moved back.

"It's not true. You know it," she said, gazing up at him. "They're framing you."

"Lily, this is a ploy by the sheriff to wrap up one murder and get rid of two Texas Rangers at the same time. Plus, if they kill Will, then you'll be available again for Matt White to marry and they will get the Sweet B."

A whirlwind blew dust along the street like a small tornado.

"How much is Jim paying you sheriff?" Seth asked. "I hope it's enough that you can hire a fine lawyer. You're going to need one."

Jim White stepped out of a building down the street. "Sheriff. Good work. You caught them."

Rage filled Will and it was all he could do to keep from pulling out his gun and shooting the man, but he knew that would endanger the others.

"We're working on it," the sheriff said.

"What's the evidence you have that I killed Tomas Garza?" Seth asked. "I'm the one who told you Will and I found the body. Why would a murderer notify the sheriff they located a dead body? This doesn't make sense and I will guarantee you the Texas Rangers will arrive once they learn what's happened to us."

The sheriff looked worried and Will could see he was trying to look strong, when he really only wanted to run.

Jim White walked into the middle of the street and gazed at Calvin who sat on his horse and then Will. "My sons. Both of your mothers were so easy to deceive. They thought I would marry them, and they were wrong."

Will didn't acknowledge the man. This piece of garbage standing in the street was not his father.

"What happened to Matt's mother," Calvin asked. "He told me she suddenly died. What did you do to her?"

Jim yanked his gun out of his holster as smooth as silk and fired a shot at Calvin, hitting him in the arm.

"Mind your own business. She died of natural causes," he said. "Consumption or pneumonia. Who knows? The woman hated living in Blessing."

The sheriff's eyes widened. "Jim, you just shot your own son."

"His mother was a whore," he said.

Calvin leaned over the saddle, trying not to groan as blood trickled down his arm.

"At least she didn't cheat people out of their money. Hire people to rob the bank, threaten people who wouldn't sell their business," Calvin said and then spit at the man.

"Shut up or you'll get another bullet," he said.

Will didn't say a word but kept looking for an opportunity to use his weapon. At this point, he wasn't opposed to shooting Jim White as long as he didn't endanger Lily or Seth.

"Arrest them, Sheriff. The court is ready to try them. We could be done with this nonsense by this afternoon."

The sheriff appeared uneasy and Will gazed at him. The man didn't want to approach them, because he knew there would be a fight. He stared at the man and laid his hand on his weapon.

"Don't do it, Sheriff. Not unless you're ready to die."

The man licked his lips and finally, he stepped around the whiskey barrels. "Get off your horses and come peacefully."

The man approached them but stopped just in front of

their horses. His face was red and Will knew he was afraid.

"No," Lily said. "They have not done anything wrong. You men know you're doing wrong. These men are Texas Rangers. There will be repercussions and you could all go to prison or face the noose because you killed innocent men."

"Shut up," Jim said. "Or I'll shoot you myself."

The man swung his gun around and pointed it at Lily.

"You're an evil snake," she said to him. "Rot in hell."

"Lily, get back," Will said. God, the woman had yet to learn how to obey him. While she thought she was protecting them, she was only causing more drama. More chances of someone besides Calvin getting hurt.

"People of Blessing," she screamed ignoring Will. "Is this how you want to continue living? With Jim White charging you higher prices. Taking your business, robbing your bank? Killing innocents? Stand up or forever live under his rule."

Suddenly shop windows opened and rifles appeared in the windows, store owners stood in the doorways with guns pointed at Jim White and the sheriff.

"You bitch," Jim said, raising his gun. "I should have killed you a long time ago."

He raised his gun and out of the corner of her eye, Will saw a pistol flash and heard a boom. Seth fired his weapon striking Jim in the center of his chest. The man fell to the ground.

Will pulled out his gun and pointed it at the men behind the whiskey barrels. The men suddenly dropped their weapons including the sheriff.

"It's over," the sheriff said. "He gave me no choice, but to arrest you."

"And because you're a weak man, you're going to resign as sheriff," Seth said, pointing his pistol at him.

"Yes, sir," he replied.

"Anyone else want a bullet. Because I'm not feeling very comfortable right now here in Blessing," Seth said.

Shocked Will gazed at the man who had fathered him lying in the street dead, the only feeling he felt was relief. Relief that he was dead.

A group of riders came thundering down the street and Will sighed with relief recognizing a group of Texas Rangers.

"You're a little late, but still a welcome sight," he said to the man he'd called captain for many years.

"We came as soon as we received your telegram. Looks like we missed all the action," Captain Clark Bell said.

The sheriff's eyes widened and he looked frightened.

"Now you can stick around and help clean up the town," Seth said. "Starting with Calvin Smith, who is the last man left from the Mercardo gang. But I will put in a good word for him. He tried to stop was going on here today. Took a bullet because of his words."

The captain took his reins from Seth. "Get some rest. We've got everything under control here. Men spread out and round up the men behind the barrels, including the sheriff."

"Captain, the shopkeepers are on our side. Leave them be. They were trying to help us."

The man nodded. "Will do. Now go get some rest and we'll talk soon."

Lily stepped into her stirrups and climbed on the back of her horse. Will knew that she would suffer punishment for taking such a risk. Yet, he was also proud of the way she tried to defend them.

But they didn't need defending. They were her men. Her protectors and they were the ones who took care of her.

With a kick to their horses, they headed for home.

23

Lily

The ride home was quiet and she could feel the tension in the air. They should be happy. They had stopped Jim White for good. There was no more danger and yet she feared they were angry with her for trying to defend her husbands.

When they rode out of town, the people cheered and yet she could tell that something was wrong. All she wanted to do now was celebrate with her men, but they were being quiet. Way too quiet.

On the ride home, all she could think about was now the Sweet B would forever be their ranch. That no one would steal it from them and that they could raise their children in the same home she grew up in.

As they rode up the drive, tears came to her eyes as she thought of her loved ones that had been taken from her. No more death. Now was the time to celebrate.

When they reached the house, Will helped her from her horse.

"Go in the house, go upstairs, strip and wait for us," he said.

That didn't sound good. They should be celebrating the end of Jim White's tyranny. They should be celebrating that they were no longer in danger.

"What's wrong?"

"Go in the house, Lily," Seth said.

With a whirl, she flounced into the house. Why did they always have to be in control? Part of her wanted to rebel and the other part knew she better do as they said or she could find herself in even more trouble.

She removed her clothes, got on the bed and laid her forehead on her hands. In this position, with her ass up in the air, she waited for them. Anxious and yet now that she was in this position, she was also excited to think about their cocks entering her pussy.

In a moment, she heard their boots on the stairs and them talking low. They were up to something and she wasn't sure she was going to like it.

When they came in, she snuck a peek as they began to remove their clothing. The expressions on their faces was not one of happiness or even joy.

"Why are you mad?" she asked, knowing she was in trouble.

"Did you put yourself at risk today?" Seth asked.

"I was protecting you," she said. "We were in this together."

There was silence and she knew they were not agreeing with her.

When they were both naked, Will sat and pulled her onto his lap. "We are your men. We protect you. You are not to ever again, get involved in the middle of a shootout. Do you understand me?"

He was angry. In fact, his dark eyes were furious.

"But—"

"How do you think we would have felt if something happened to you today?"

How could they misconstrue something so badly? All she had wanted to do was protect them, stop the sheriff and even Jim White from harming her men.

"He was going to arrest you for a murder we know you didn't commit. You're my men. Of course, I'm going to stand up for you. Just like you stand up for me."

Seth took her and placed her over his knee.

Smack! His palm hit her cheeks and not in an easy, playful manner.

Smack! "Don't you ever get between us and the sheriff ever again. We could handle the situation without your help. All you did was endanger all of us, when you got off your horse and started toward them."

Smack! Fire radiated from her cheeks as tears welled in her eyes.

"Do you understand why we're upset?" Will asked.

"No, I only wanted to protect the two of you," she said. "How do you think my life would be without you here by my side. I can't go through being all alone again. You are my men, my life."

Smack! Seth's palm connected once again.

This time she could not hold back the tears any longer. They rolled down her cheeks.

Seth raised her and cradled her on his lap.

"You must obey us, for your own safety," he said.

She sobbed on his shoulder and he rubbed her back. "You are my men. I love you and would die protecting you."

Seth leaned back and kissed her on the mouth, his lips moving over hers in a gentle way. Then he released her and gazed in her eyes. "I love you with all my heart and you scared me today. When those men cocked their guns, I thought we were all going to die, because I would never let a single one of them live, if they killed you."

She leaned her head against his shoulder and hugged him.

Then he passed her to Will. "Honey, I love you and you scared me so badly. Never do that again."

She hiccupped. "I'm sorry, I frightened you, but I was fighting mad and wanted to protect the love we have."

"Let us do the protecting," Seth said.

"Yes, or you'll be spanked again," Will promised.

"Seth, you really spanked me."

"Yes, I did. But I would never harm you. Does it hurt?"

What could she say? It burned a little, but there was a fire raging inside her that he'd created.

"A little, but mainly you made me want you so badly, I can't stand it."

Seth put his fingers between her legs and up her cunny.

"She's soaking wet," he said with a grin. "Oh, honey, I love that you get so excited."

Will kissed her, his mouth moving over hers, causing her to groan with need.

When they broke apart, he gazed at her. "On your knees."

On the bed she crawled onto her knees. With a quick glance behind her, she saw Seth had another plug and was greasing it up.

"The last one," he said. "In fact, I think we both take you tonight."

The thought was both chilling and thrilling and she

couldn't wait to experience what it would feel like with both her strong, handsome men claiming her at the same time.

Will pushed her head down on the bed, raising her bottom into the air. His fingers slid into her bottom so easily now, sending a tingle through her, causing her to gasp. Stroking her insides, she whimpered as he filled her with his fingers, stretching her, a rush of pure heat spiraled through her.

A moan escaped from her as he slowly pushed the largest plug into her bottom and gasped as the wooden dowel slipped inside her.

Will stroked his cock near her face. "Lily, suck me."

She opened her mouth and lovingly sucked the end of his cock, her tongue circling it. Seth was behind her and she glanced back to see him spreading her legs.

His fingers brushed against her clit and she almost came then. Between the spanking, the butt plug, and now his fingers pushing her closer and closer to the edge, she knew she wouldn't last long.

With Will's cock in her mouth, she groaned as Seth continued to stroke her. Will reached down and twisted her nipples and she gazed up at him, with his cock in her mouth.

They were her men. Her protectors, her lovers, and her husbands, and she loved them with every fiber of her being. They were her reasons for living.

Seth twisted the butt plug and she all but screamed on Will's cock as heat flooded her and she moved her ass begging him for more.

"Oh, Lily, I'm going to come," Will said. "Swallow it all."

At that moment, she felt him surge in her throat and she swallowed his seed as it pulsed inside her throat and she licked his cock as it slipped from her mouth.

Seth plunged into her pussy and she clenched her muscles around his girth, wanting it, needing it, inside her. Ripples of pleasure spread through her and she knew that if she came, she would be in trouble.

Will moved beneath her and she knew they were preparing to take her both at the same time.

She felt Seth pull the plug partially out and then he rammed it back in.

"Seth," she cried. "Please, I'm going to come."

"Not yet," he said.

Will was stroking his cock and she could see that it was getting hard again and she knew he was going to put it in her pussy.

Seth pulled out of her pussy and then he pulled the plug. She felt empty, bereft.

Glancing back over her shoulder, she wanted to beg him. "Seth, I feel so empty."

"Not for long, darling," he said.

His penis was at her arse. They were truly going to take her, both at the same time. Fear and desire mixed through her and she felt him pushing. Without thinking, she tensed.

"Let me in, Lily. Open for me," Seth said, stroking her clit.

She sighed and relaxed against Will's chest as Seth pushed his cock into her, filling her. He was so big and even though they had prepared her, she felt like she was being ripped in two.

"It's too big, Seth," she cried.

"A little more, darling, a little more and then you'll be all ours. We're going to fuck you and make you ours."

She took a deep breath and tried to relax. Suddenly she felt Seth glide the rest of the way in and his hips were against her buttocks.

"Oh," she cried, trying her best to relax.

"Now my turn," Will said as he pushed into her pussy.

They were both inside her and she felt stuffed. These were her men, her lovers, and she loved that they were both claiming her. Now she was truly theirs.

"Darling, your ass is so tight. It feels so good," Seth told her as he pulled out and then in again.

Will begin to pull out when Seth was going in. They began a rhythm, with one going in and the other one pulling out. Will reached up and sucked her nipple into his mouth, his teeth nipping her puckered bud.

The bed began to move and Lily felt like she would explode as the passion consumed her. The flames were burning her as she rocked with their bodies.

"Seth, Will," she cried as the heat begin to spiral through her, the walls of her pussy clenching. "Fuck me."

Never did she imagine that being taken by them both would leave her feeling so out of control, like any moment, she would melt right here in their arms.

"Now your ours," Will said, his voice rough. "You belong to us. Only us."

"Yes," she cried. "I'm yours. I'm going to come."

"Go ahead, darling, you deserve it," Seth said as he popped her on the buttocks, sending her over the edge.

With a scream, she felt her insides tighten and her muscles ripple around their cocks. "Oh, Seth, Will."

"Yes," Seth said. "Grip my cock with your muscles."

Will pushed deep, spasming inside her as his seed coated the walls of her pussy.

"Lily," he groaned.

Seth slapped her on the ass once again and this time she

felt him slam into her, his seed coating her, groaning as he leaned over her.

"You're ours," he said as he convulsed around her.

The smell of sex filled the room as they all three collapsed. Lily lay between her cowboys. How had she gotten so lucky? They had ridden into her life and rescued her and yet in some ways, she felt like she rescued them.

"That was fantastic," she said.

"Yes," Will agreed.

"Rest and we'll do it again," Seth said.

Lying between them, all she could think about was that today, they had confessed their love for one another. "You're my cowboys," she said. "And I love you."

Sure, they would face other dangers, but they had each other.

24

Ten months later

The two men paced the floor downstairs, their boots making a clunking noise on the wooden floor.

"About damn time you got back," Will said. "She's been looking out the window every day watching for you."

Seth frowned at his friend, his brother, the man he shared a wife with. "I hurried. You know how long it takes to catch a bank robber. It was my last case. I'm home for good."

Will glanced up the stairs. "Thank goodness for that. Taking care of Lily, watching her grow bigger every day, wondering if you were going to be here or not for the birth, was driving her crazy."

And Will crazy. A pregnant woman was not the easiest woman to get along with.

A scream rent the air and both men shivered.

"I can't do this again," Will said. "Not alone. You have to be here."

Seth grinned. "She was that hard to handle?"

Oh, he didn't even know the half of it. The cravings for weird foods and then the tears, the laughter, the feeling of his son or daughter moving in her belly. So many emotions and yet who was he kidding. He couldn't wait to get her pregnant again.

"You know how stubborn she can be. She wanted us to have sex night before last."

"And you turned her down?"

"Well, with our son or daughter right there, I didn't think it was a good idea. So I gave her some relief with my fingers," he said. The very idea of fucking his very pregnant wife was weird. Not that she wasn't beautiful. In fact, in many ways, pregnancy had made her radiant.

Another scream rent the air and they both looked at one another and then took the stairs two at a time. They had to make certain she was all right.

"I don't give a damn what that midwife says. This ain't right. Somethings wrong," Seth said.

"What if she's dying? We can't lose her," Will said, fear clutching his chest, his breathing accelerating. Women died in labor and he couldn't live without Lily.

They threw open the door to see the midwife down between their wife's legs.

"Gentlemen, it's a boy," she said with a grin.

Will glanced at the squirming baby and then he ran to Lily's side.

"Are you all right?"

She grinned. "Tired, but we have a son."

The midwife handed the knife to Seth. "Would you like to cut the umbilical cord?"

"Yes," he said and sliced through the cord.

While the midwife delivered the afterbirth, Seth took his

son in his arms. "Hey, little man. Welcome to our world. You are so very loved."

"Let me hold him," Lily said.

Seth took their child and kneeled beside his wife. "Our family."

Tears flowed down her cheeks. "If you don't mind, I'd like to name him after my father. The next one can be named by you."

Seth and Will nodded and then they gazed at their son. Each man kissed her on the lips. "Thank you."

"Yes, thank you for creating our family."

Lily smiled. "I love you, my cowboys."

"And we love you," they both said.

***

I'm so glad that Lily, Seth and Will found happiness and created a family. Sorry, but I'm a sucker for showing the family together at the end. I truly hope you enjoyed this book. Please be sure to leave a review.

Be sure to follow me on Bookbub by clicking https://www.bookbub.com/authors/lacey-davis.

Thanks again for reading. Next up is Two Cowboys' Christmas Bride. Here's an excerpt.

Two Cowboys' Christmas Bride

Anna Best never dreamed her life could go so wrong. Two weeks before Christmas, her uncle sold her to the local whorehouse. One evening before the madam of the house could sell off her virginity, she'd been drugged and abducted.

Now she found herself in a rough tow sack that smelled

like potatoes being hauled around in the back of a wagon. Whoever opened this bag better be prepared, because she would come out fighting.

Anna was no simpering woman and she was aching to give a good tongue lashing. The bouncing of the wagon had jolted her awake to her head pounding, her wrists tied, her mouth covered, and stuffed in a bag.

Not exactly how she'd planned her escape from the brothel.

The wagon wheels came to a stop and she listened as two voices whispered in the darkness.

"Is this the right place," a female voice said.

"I think so," a young man said.

"Come on, lift her out of the wagon and let's leave her on the doorstep."

Anna wanted to scream, but all she could do was make muted noises. Still, she could kick.

"Good thing you stuffed her mouth, Ma."

Ma? A woman was involved in her kidnapping?

Fury roared through her as they dragged the gunnysack along the back of the wagon. She kicked and flailed her legs trying to create as much havoc for them as possible.

"Stop moving, girl, or I will drop you right here in the dirt," the woman said quietly.

Where did she know that voice from?

Tiring, she stopped thrashing as they carried her then set her down on the cold ground.

"Let's go," the woman whispered in the darkness.

"Won't she freeze to death?" a young male voice asked.

"Not this one. The devil is strong within her," the woman said.

What? Did the woman believe she wanted to be taken to a

whorehouse? To have her uncle, a family member, sell her? All she had asked for in life was a loving family. And look where that had gotten her.

Sold to a brothel.

As they walked away, the sounds of their retreating footsteps crunching on the ground sent fear slamming into Anna. Trembling, she lay balled up in the darkness, unable to discern where they left her. What if wild wolves or coyotes found her?

What if she died right here inside this bag?

The cold started to creep into the potato sack. In Blessing, Texas, the winters were mild, but still she started to shake. It was December, not exactly a hot summer day.

Doubled over inside the bag, she didn't have room to stretch her legs and they were going numb. She rolled and came up against a hard surface. A barn? House?

Rocking inside the bag, she hit the wall.

Bang!

Did anyone live here? Did she want to find out?

Bang.

Bang.

Tiring, her shoulder throbbing, she heard a noise.

A door opened.

"What the hell?"

"Hold that lantern a little higher, Mack," a voice said.

"What's the note say?" a deeper male voice asked.

"Merry Christmas."

Anna's temper exploded. She writhed and screamed as much as she could inside the bag.

The men cursed. "Someone's in there."

With relief, she felt them untying the bag and pulling it

down then lifting her to her numb feet. Her eyes were blinded by the light of the lantern.

"Oh my God, it's a woman."

"A damn fine-looking woman," the other man said.

Slowly her eyes adjusted to the light as she stared at two extremely handsome men standing in the doorway without shirts on. Muscled arms and chests with wisps of dark hair glowed in the warm light.

Who were these men and why had she been delivered here?

"Santa brought us an early Christmas present. A woman."

TWO COWBOYS
CHRISTMAS
BRIDE

LACEY DAVIS

PLEASE LEAVE A REVIEW

Did you enjoy the book? Reviews help authors. I would appreciate you posting a review. https://www.amazon.com/review/create-review/error?ie=UTF8&channel=glance-detail&asin=B08KHTDTQ9

Follow Lacey on Facebook at http://facebook.com/LaceyDavisromancewriter

Sign up for my new book alert here https://www.subscribepage.com/laceydavis_author and receive a complimentary book.

Also By Lacey Davis

Blessing, Texas Series
Loving My Cowboys
Two Cowboys' Christmas Bride
Two Cowboys One Bride
Two Cowboys Too Perfect
Two Cowboys to Protect Her
Two Cowboys Save Christmas

Bridgewater Brides World
Their Perfect Bride
Their Tempting Bride
Their Scandalous Bride

Treasure Falls Brides
Our Fugitive Bride
Our Desperate Bride
Our Wild Bride

Want to learn about my new releases before anyone else?
Sign up for my New Book Alert and receive a
complimentary book. Blindfold Me.

ABOUT THE AUTHOR

Lacey Davis is a pseudonym for a USA Today bestselling author who wanted to try her hand at writing sexy romance. With these novels, I hope to write sizzling romances that will leave you grabbing a fan to cool yourself off.

If you like hunky bad boy heroes who like to be in charge and strong pretty women who are willing to risk it all, then look no further. These sexy reads will get you in the mood. Come experience strong women who will tame these bad boys and leave them wanting more.

The End